I ALWAYS WIN

JILL SHAKLEY

 FriesenPress

Suite 300 - 990 Fort St
Victoria, BC, V8V 3K2
Canada

www.friesenpress.com

ISBN
978-1-5255-9145-7 (Hardcover)
978-1-5255-9144-0 (Paperback)
978-1-5255-9146-4 (eBook)

1. FICTION, ACTION & ADVENTURE

Distributed to the trade by The Ingram Book Company

ACKNOWLEDGEMENTS

PROFOUND THANKS, AS EVER, GO TO OUR GALLANT first reader, Vivian Campbell, adept at pointing out strengths as well as weaknesses. A special thank you to Lancashire scholar Michael Higgins and his wife Susan. Any remaining mistakes are ours. Without the support of dear, patient Carly and her colleagues at FriesenPress, of course, there would be no book. Thank you all.

CHAPTER

— 1 —

As, footsore, I plodded the dirty, sordid London streets, a foul wind blew old, yellowed newspapers about raggedly clad children who sat starving in the gutters. All about me I found filth and disgusting vileness. Sickened, I limped my way to the opium den.

Well, unfortunately, to be more accurate, it was a beautiful day with a cloudless sky, a brilliant sun, and only a slight breeze from the north to cool my face. The children were playing hopscotch on the other side of the road amid shrill cries of delight. Two of the boys looked rather pudgy, and one of the girls had an all-day sucker. They might have owed the shabbiness of their clothes to the worldwide Depression, but in my experience an active child can destroy the newest, most expensive apparel in seconds.

My objective was also a disappointment: a pub where a bunch of us not-yet-famous artists and writers had an informal club; that is, we each put up tuppence per year to pay for the book, the ink, and the pen for the secretary-treasurer-president to put our names in a list. Well, at least we belonged to something, and this place had really good beef sandwiches, and a not bad red wine, both cheap. The place itself was not in the best repair and was not spotless or well lit. We called it The Frozen Inkpot. Others called it The Missing Jackpot.

When I entered, the pub was full of men of various ages, none of them much better dressed than the children outside. Each of the comparatively few women was individual in appearance, but they fell into two major categories. A couple were heavy and well-muscled, more just heavy. A few were thin with lots of beads. All smoked. I wished I could afford the luxury. I was limited to two coffin nails per diem.

Six months before, I had gone to Paris. Just

out of school, I knew I was destined to be a writer, and I felt Paris was the place to get started. I had heard of people doing great things there. I was not one of them. Even living as cheaply as possible and not eating more than once a day, I still could not make my bit of money last long. Worse, I did no real writing. I did try to start. I later heard that I'd missed the zenith of the arts in Paris by several years.

I could not earn any money there. My schoolboy French was so slight, I could not get the merest of jobs, so before I went totally broke, I took a boat back to London, hoping to get work at something and write a bit at night.

The Depression, however, had made any job hard to find. You really had to know someone just to get your foot in the door. At present the outlook was not bright; however, the call of destiny still pulled me on.

As a corrective to my determined optimism, there over at a corner table sat William, sometime actor and master of accents. William said he'd been a coal miner in Wales. I'd heard that he had in fact applied for the job but was let go after a couple of hours. He had a scruffy, dark brown beard and a football scarf; I couldn't guess the team. I went over and sat down with him.

"How's tricks?" I asked.

"Not too good. I'm trying to write a poem about sewers, but it just won't come."

"Oh, that's nice," I said, to encourage artistic fever.

"Aye. I tried to change it to a cesspool, but I don't think most people have ever seen one. There aren't many about nowadays."

He sounded profoundly regretful. Mind you, I've always thought that London accents have a hard edge to them that gives a negative sound to the most cheerful comment. I had found that, once I'd mastered that London sound, I could pass as a native. No one believed I'd come from his exact neighbourhood, but that was safer, anyway. I wouldn't have to pretend I knew old Ted Allworthy or Jack Potter. Although he did sometimes venture into rhyming slang, William usually had one of the more respectable London accents.

"True," I said. "Yes, I see your point. So we return to sewers."

"Did you go down into the sewers of Paris when you were there?"

"No," I admitted. "I never found my way in. To tell the truth my French is not too good in the real world. They talk so fast in Paris, and there are a lot of different accents."

"Right. I see. Difficult."

"I heard you had a job writing something."

"Oh, well," William replied. "For five weeks I did. This high hat was paying me five quid a week to write the history of his family. I do have the qualifications to do it. I got Don—the Irish artist—to do them up for me with real signatures, seals, and all. Looked great, and what's more important, they passed muster."

"So you're doing that now?"

"Nope. I was doing great. The people at the British Museum and such the like really did a lot of the hard part, finding stuff for me. I just had to copy it out and make it sound nice. Then in the 1640s, I got the Order of the Boot."

"But you made twenty-five pounds out of it."

"Yes, except that I had to pay the Irish chap a cut for his work doing the documents. But I still have them, so I may get a chance to use them again."

"Well, you sound like they could be yours anyway."

And, I thought, for that matter, they could be mine, perhaps even more convincingly.

"So what are you going to do, now that you're out of it again?"

"Well, I know a little about cars, so I could try that. I did try being a valet for a while, but it paid nothing, and I didn't have much time of my own for my real work: describing present-day England to the masses in verse."

I had no such well-defined objective yet, even in my head. In fact, at the moment I was rather aimless. It makes you feel like one of those useless mouths you read about in a socialist paper.

"What's a valet do, anyway?" I asked.

"Not too much. He keeps the great lord's clothing cleaned, pressed, and folded away, makes sure the boots and shoes are cleaned, the top of his cane polished, the shaving things set up right: things he could do himself, if he wasn't a lazy sod. Some toffs even have their man shave them."

"But mostly you have to know how to take care of clothes?" I asked.

"Well, yes. We had to at school."

"Oh. Right. You went to one of them. I forgot."

"Have you ever shaved anyone?" he asked.

"Yes."

"With a straight razor?"

"Yes," I told him. "I had to shave my dad, when he broke his arm. He had a beard when he was an officer in the Royal Navy, but I think Mom didn't like it around the house, so she insisted he shave it off. Funny. When he hurt his arm, she wouldn't shave him, so I had to learn. It may prove useful one day, I guess."

"How about *Stench* for a title?" William suggested.

"Hasn't it been used?"

"Oh, hell! I don't want something already used. What about *Filth* instead? Wait! What about—No, they wouldn't print that. Are you sure about *Stench*?"

"Fairly certain."

"You see: I have this grand idea. Call it a Vision. But I don't know what it is or how to explain it. Language is such a limited way."

"Well, what about painting or music?"

"I am no artist or composer," he said.

"That's the trouble," I agreed. "Life keeps coming to these bleak endings. Wait! That's it: *Bleak Ending*!" I pronounced.

"Wonderful! That's real artistic expressionism."

"I never heard of that before."

"No, I just invented it."

"Mind if I use it?"

"No, help yourself."

"Aren't there any jobs out there?" I pursued.

"Well, there is this Depression thing going on. Say, though: if you can drive a team of four, you could get a job with one of the brewing companies. I heard they were a bit short on drivers."

"No, I've never driven even one horse."

"Odd, you know," William reflected. "Not too long ago there would have been lots of men, but now they all drive lorries and cabs, the ones that have motors."

"I assume they don't need any street-sweepers?"

"No, there's a queue for those sorts of jobs. Right now: no special skill, no work."

I thought about it. I did like a cigarette now and then. I didn't want to smoke a pipe like my father, who moved about like a one-stack battleship. Looking around at the poorly dressed, rather D-grade crowd in this temple of the arts, I was not too impressed; however, it might form the basis for a story I could write, if I could think of a story and then could write it. I did have pens and ink and paper, an essential starting point. Now just for the gentle push to get a tale out of these geniuses.

There was a little paper called *The Penny Delight* that would buy stuff, if it was written clearly on one side of the paper or, better, typed, but I had no typewriter, and I had yet to learn. The future of writing seemed to be heading in that direction in a forceful way. Even the select few writers who were above flogging their stuff around low-life publications had to hire typists to sort out their work for the big-time press people.

The Penny Delight was a bit farther down. They printed short stories such as murder mysteries, and articles such as how to lace your tennis shoes so as to improve your game: delightful and/or practical, a good little sheet. I had noticed mostly women reading it, but I assumed men did, too.

We bought a beef sandwich, which we cut in half, and one small glass of rather sweet wine each. Afterward, I felt a bit better, but it did not solve the problem of how to pay for, or at least acquire, my next sandwich.

A small voice said, "I always win."

You might think it would be understandable to feel some alarm at hearing voices in your head. Look what happened to Joan of Arc. I was used to it, however, and it was only the one voice. The first time I heard it was on the occasion of an end-of-term lucky draw at school for a book prize. The volume in question was *Creative Writing for Young People* by Ann Merrit. I'm not certain why I wanted that book. Sheer childish single-mindedness, I suppose. I'd never won anything before. I don't think any of my schoolmates really wanted it. I could probably have convinced the winner to give it to me, or I could have asked my mother to buy me a copy. Anyway, silly or not, I really did want that book. Just before the draw, I heard a voice say, "I always win," and I did. It seemed natural at the time.

After that I heard it at irregular intervals over the years. It never said anything else, and it wasn't always so immediately right. I wasn't even positive it was always right at all. I mean, we all have so many things going on all the time in our lives, some good and some bad, it might have just been chance.

Oh, yes: the book. I read it, and it convinced me that I wanted to be a writer. I hadn't had any long-range goals before, but the author made the creative process seem like a cozy sort of magic. She never said it was easy. In retrospect, the sternness of her rules and admonishments probably intimidated me—certainly not her intention. Her central message was that anyone willing to apply himself adequately could write, that it was something you did, not something that struck you effortlessly, like lightning. Too bad; that would have been a lot easier.

CHAPTER
— 2 —

I SAID GOOD NIGHT TO WILLIAM AND THE MOB and trudged home—in my case a cupboard on the third floor of an old house full of small rented rooms. Mine contained a bed, a chair, and a lamp, the only light. Mrs. Bleary, my land-lady, had assured me that having no window to let in cold air was an advantage for which she should charge extra.

Some of her flock, like me, were simple lodgers. The boarders were an elite class; they paid for two meals a day. I could not aspire to that. At present my main concern about shelter was how to raise next week's rent. I did not have it.

Could I get a job at one of the big hotels? Then I thought: what about a liner, sort of a floating hotel? They'd have to provide room and board for the crew, even the lowly cabin stewards. Hmm..

I went downstairs and checked through the telephone directories for addresses. I could not afford to make calls, so the next morning I went to the Cunard office. They had no openings, so I walked on to the White Star Line. There I got only a "'Op it, mate," with a finger pointing to the door in case I couldn't see it.

Not encouraging, but only two down. I continued on to the P&O Line. They were either too proud or too busy to see me at all.

Feeling slightly defeated, with nothing to show for a morning's wear and tear on shoe leather, I had started back to Mrs. Bleary's when I saw in the window of a sweet shop a sign requiring various kinds of domestic help. William had said that was a fairly soft go. Why not give it a try?

I hastened back to my room. I got out my good suit and shaved again. Then I took great care to comb my hair with the part fashionably in the middle. Taking a deep breath, I returned to the place I had targeted.

The street door opened onto a flight of stairs that took me up to a shabby waiting room, like The Frozen Inkpot full of more men than women, but these were all just staring like waxworks.

The clerk at the desk beckoned me over. I tried to stride confidently forward.

"Name?" he asked.

"Goodale, Rodney A." I gave him my London voice.

"Just have a chair. We'll get around to you."

I sat. The place had nothing to read, so I joined the staring waxworks brigade. Every so often a person would reply to his name and enter the office of the big boss, or tomato sauce, as William would have labelled him in rhyming slang.

In speaking of getting around to me, the clerk should have added: "in the fullness of time." Mind you, the wait probably seemed longer than it was. Don't they always?

Eventually he called out: "Goodale!" and glanced around at us, having already forgotten which one I was. When I stood, he announced,

"He will see you now," as if it were an audience with the king.

The boss's name was on the door, but I passed through too quickly to read the small gold letters properly. It looked like Blinkingsod, not very likely. Still, I never found out any different, so he'll have to remain Blinkingsod. He sat going through papers at a worn desk in an unclean office. The windows must have been washed last about the time of the Siege of Sebastopol. Perhaps that was as well. I wasn't impressed enough to be nervous.

The balding, hawk-nosed man regarded me through large pince-nez specs and motioned me to a chair.

"Good lord!" he said. "Who told you I was fielding a rugby team? You're too young and too big. No one wants footmen now. Well, there is one chance."

After a few minutes' search he found the papers he was looking for.

"Right," he declared. "Here it is." He held up a form of some kind as if it were a two-foot trout. "I couldn't remember the gentleman's name. I should have. He's hired a lot of staff from us.

They don't stay with him long."

That didn't sound encouraging.

"He is not overly concerned with appearance, but he needs someone who is—shall we say?—a bit up-market when he talks."

Oops. I'd started off wrong then. I relaxed and let her rip in my normal fashion.

"I take it that the gentleman requires a person who speaks properly."

"Good," Mr. Blinkingsod nodded. "Just like the real thing. Can you keep up the posh talk, or was that it?"

"Oh, I believe I can maintain this manner of speech, sir. May I ask what he needs me for?"

"The Honourable Frederick Oglethorpe needs a valet. The problem is that he cannot, even for a short time, stand to listen to what we may call common speech. I don't suppose you have had any experience as a valet?"

"I should be adequate in the role," I claimed. "I have done such a job before, but I haven't brought my letters of recommendation with me. I had not planned to come here. It was a fortuitous happening."

I hoped William knew where Don the Irish

artist was at the moment. It looked as if I'd need his skill at documentation. It should have occurred to me that a prospective employer would want references.

"Forget it," he said to my relief. "He won't ask for any papers. Places no stock in references. I like the way you can keep up the chat. Very good."

"Thank you, sir."

"He's staying at the Hotel Clarion. I'll write out the address for you, and I'll call him to say you're coming. Yes, I think you may do for him—at least for a while."

He wrote down the name and address and handed the paper to me.

"Well, off you go."

Surprised, I went past the staring unemployed creatures and the clerk, down the stairs, and into the street, where there was oxygen. I hadn't noticed at the time, but in that dingy place the air had all been breathed up.

With that interview behind me, I faced a new problem. The address of my prospective employer was quite a distance away. I had no money for the Underground, and no one I knew could give me a lift. I sat down on a step and wondered whether I should bother to pursue this any further. After all, if this blighter Oglethorpe gave his valets the boot after such a short time, how would that help me? Would I be any different, posh speech or not?

"Yes," said a voice in my head. "I always win."

I retied my shoes and straightened my socks. It was a long march, but it had to be done somehow. My destiny and destination were to be the same; they were bound up together. I checked this out by flipping my last farthing. It came up heads. I marched.

CHAPTER
— 3 —

I STRODE FORTH HEROICALLY. ON SUCH A LONG walk, many would have fallen by the wayside. Not me. I was made of sterner stuff. Still, I could not help reflecting that it was getting to be a bit much. I mean, it was a bloody long way to go, simply to see if I might get work. The bloke could just not like my face or something. He did sound, well, like a bit of a nutter.

Repeatedly stifling my misgivings, I strode across the great city and finally came up to the Clarion. It was not a big, expensive sort of place, which made me a bit concerned. Could this chap afford to pay much? After all the walking I'd done, I was going to need a new pair of shoes soon, or at least to get these resoled.

I crossed the street and sat down in the lobby of the hotel for a bit of a rest. Then I scouted out a mirror in the main hall and made sure I looked fit for work. I was especially concerned that my hair looked nice and that I still had that middle part that looks so slick.

Now appearing less bedraggled, I stepped over to the desk and asked the chap behind it to inform the Honourable Frederick that I was here and would appreciate an audience. He complied at once and told me to take the lift to 304. At least I really was expected.

The lift boy, a tall, dark young chap, seemed to read my destination and purpose, for as I exited he said, "Good luck, mate," in a sceptical tone. Although this did not raise my spirits, I thanked him with an airy wave of the hand.

I expected to have to scout around for Room 304, but the door stood directly across the corridor from the lift. In fact, it was the only door I could see, which argued accommodations huger than just a room, perhaps a large suite. This was more like it.

I knocked in a robust but gentlemanly

fashion. After a short wait the door opened, bringing me face to face with an elegantly but unostentatiously dressed man of medium build. He had slightly greying hair with a more than slightly greying mustache, full but of the army officer type. In fact, that was his general appearance altogether.

He greeted me in a friendly manner: a good start. I decided he was younger than the colour of his hair suggested, perhaps thirty-five or so.

"Well, come in. The agency said you were on your way, so I expected you earlier."

On impulse, I decided to be straight with him, at least up to a point.

"I regret to say that I had no money for transport and walked from the agency. I had not intended to apply for employment, or I would have brought my references."

He raised his grey eyebrows.

"Well, well. I must say that shows pluck and the right spirit. Much more important than pieces of paper. You're hired. What's your name?"

"Rodney Anson Goodale, sir."

"Two admirals and a brewer," he smiled, "not a bad combination, I must say. I meant what I said. When can you start?"

This was a bit more abrupt than I'd expected but fine with me. I wondered if he hired all his valets at the door.

"Well, sir," I replied, "I must return to my rooms to collect my apparel. My other things can go into storage."

I thought that sounded better than to admit that I owned nothing more than a few items of clothing in a battered second-hand suitcase. The Honourable Frederick seemed to accept what I said without a thought.

"Right. I'll give you cab fare so that you can attend to the business at once."

He pulled out a fiver, apparently the only size note he had. I accepted it with my most casual air.

"Yes, sir. Thank you, sir," I acknowledged and took off, before he could change his mind, for the great open spaces where a search should enable one to secure a cab.

I got one without assistance from the doorman, saving me the cost of a tip, and when I reached my digs, I had the driver wait. Without lingering I found Mrs. Bleary and told her the good news:

she could rent my room without waiting until the end of the week. Then I gathered up my few clothes and stuffed them into my suitcase. The cabby looked relieved to see me again. I could understand his misgivings because of the unprepossessing appearance of the dwelling place.

When we'd returned to the Clarion and I handed the cabby my fiver, he shook his head.

"Sure you ain't got nothing smaller, chum?"

"Indeed I am sure," I replied ruefully.

In his place I'd have wondered whether I'd come by it honestly, but he was entirely concerned with the immediate practical problem.

"Look, mate, I'm just starting out. Ain't got no change yet. What say I see if they can change it inside?"

"Good idea," I agreed.

He disappeared into the hotel and came out beaming: he'd got change. I gave him a sixpence tip.

Luggage in hand, I got back into the lift. The boy glanced at me and without comment returned me to 304. This was more the travel time my new employer had expected, and he admitted me faster.

CHAPTER
— 4 —

U<small>P TO THEN ALL</small> I'<small>D SEEN OF MY NEW HOME WAS</small> a patch of wall by the front door, and I can't say the pastel-flowered beige wallpaper told me much. Now I had the opportunity for a better look, and I liked what I saw. Not only was the suite even larger than I'd thought, more like a flat, but it had a homey feeling, complete with shelves of books and a nice fireplace in the living room. It smelled of pipe tobacco but not my dad's mix.

When we'd got that far in, my employer sat down; I remained standing.

"Now," he told me, picking up a pipe and gesturing with it. I was interested to see that it was a bent-stemmed briar like my dad smoked. "I have to be very careful with my money. The most I can afford to pay you is five shillings a week—plus room and board, of course."

That was not princely, but I currently had one farthing in the world. Five bob was at least money, and money I needn't pay out on food and lodging. I remember one of our literary mob saying, "Money is only really real when you don't have it." At the time I didn't understand that, but I do now.

I moved to hand the Honourable Frederick his change from the cab fare.

Standing, he laughed, "Oh, hell, keep it."

I didn't know what to say. Was he kidding? But he put down his pipe, turned his back, and said, "Follow me," so I did. The coins felt strange in my pocket.

We passed through a small dining room and a kitchen, not large either but modern. On the far side of that was a bedroom.

"This is yours," he announced. "Put away your things and then bring me a brandy and soda."

He turned again and left me. I looked around the room, comparatively huge, with a window and a clean one at that. The bed was half again as wide as I was used to and had a good mattress. There was a roomy dresser with a mirror above and a cupboard with another mirror, this one full-length, on the door. There was a floor lamp beside a well-padded armchair. I may seem to be gushing over a simple bedroom, but after Mrs. Bleary's mousehole, this was Buckingham Palace.

Quickly I unpacked my few items and hurried out to find where the beverages were kept. I thought I'd glimpsed them in the main room. I was correct. There was even a little icebox with bottles of soda water in it, and clean glasses stood nearby. Having sorted this out, I made his drink and brought it to him. At the last minute I remembered to stick it onto a silver tray.

"Not too much brandy," he cautioned me. "This stuff costs money, and I always need to watch the pennies."

Leaving him to his refresher, I completed my first tour of the suite. Past the living room, the master bedroom was distinguished from my own by a large wardrobe, a rug, and a bookcase overflowing with both fat and thin books. As a valet's principle duties involve his master's clothes, I thought I should sort through the Honourable Frederick's, but it felt wrong, so instead I went back and took a look into the kitchen cupboards and icebox. After all, I might have to prepare dinner. In addition to some basic utensils, I found bread, butter, marmalade, and eggs. Was this all that my employer ate, or was I expected to go out for groceries?

Unsure what to do, I returned to the living room, where the Honourable Frederick was sipping his drink and listening to a program on a rather super wireless set I hadn't noticed before, as it was contained in a cabinet that did not reveal its secret until the doors opened. Instead of mere headphones, the machine boasted a proper speaker. It was odd-sounding but pleasant music, with different voices coming in at different times. At the end of the piece a BBC announcer described it as "Elizabethan folk tunes." I assume he'd know.

I didn't want to interrupt my new boss, but he noticed me standing there, just inside the room.

"Oh, yes," he remarked. "I am dining out tonight."

"Very good, sir."

"You phone down to the Service Desk to tell the staff what you want. Over by the phone there's a menu card and the number to ring up."

"What about breakfast, sir?"

"Oh, I always have two soft-boiled eggs and four slices of toast. Saves money, not having it sent up."

Without waiting for me to lay out his clothes, he began to get ready to leave, but he had trouble with his tie. At last a crisis I could handle. I stepped forward.

"Please, sir, allow me."

I undid the mess and got behind him so that I could imagine putting it on myself.

"The objective, sir," I informed him, "is not to have it perfect, or it will look like a made-up tie, so we let the left side have a slightly larger loop, and we allow the right side to droop just a tiny bit, and, voilà!: a real bow tie."

He stared into the mirror oddly for a few seconds and then laughed.

"That's why that woman said I should get someone who could tie ties properly. You're hired! Well, you are already, but I had to say something, what? Well done. This may be an important night for me. Oh. Listen for the racing results at Newmarket. Find out how Glittering Lucy finished. I want to know."

He chose a dark green coat. I handed him his hat and cane, and off he went.

I wandered about until I found the menu sheet. It wasn't extensive, but I was hungry. I ordered shepherd's pie with a double helping of potatoes to fill me up.

As they knew it was just for the help, I waited for three quarters of an hour, and it was brought in by the lift boy.

"Got the job, eh, mate?" he grinned.

"Yes," I replied, steering clear of too friendly a manner but also leaving it open.

He nodded as if he'd had a hand in it and waved as he left the room. He was a very likable chap.

I realized that I was not really up on the below-stairs etiquette and would have to learn quickly because it was part of the trade. After I'd devoured my meal, I turned on the wireless, but they didn't give the race results, just dance music. Blast.

I wasn't a follower of the races, but back in my

own part of town, I'd have known how to find out. Here I was a stranger. Suddenly, I had an idea. I stepped out and summoned the lift. It arrived with the food-deliverer still at the helm.

"What now, mate?" he asked.

"How can I find out today's race results from Newmarket?"

"No prob. Go down and ask Sammy, the doorman. You seen him: lookin' like a bleeding general out front."

"Oh, right. Thank you."

I did indeed remember him, the person I'd done my best to avoid earlier. Now he was easy to find. A great fellow, he had all the racing stuff and gave me the dope, as he called it, in a flash.

"Lookin' to have a bit on for tomorrow?" he asked.

I realized he must be the local bookies' helper.

"Well, not right now, but I will not forget where you are, if the need does arise," I assured him with a friendly smile.

He wouldn't expect a tip from the help, and I wasn't sure what to give him anyway. You learn these things over time.

I returned upstairs and wrote down that

Glittering Lucy had won by a short head, whatever that meant. Then I set down the note by the drinks tray. I did not succumb to the temptation to have one in case he marked the bottles. Some chaps do that.

I noticed a full ashtray on the rather untidy table beside my employer's chair and straightened up the mess. I ran an eye down the nearby bookcase. The titles meant nothing to me except that many sounded military. There was one set of thirteen red volumes of uneven sizes: *A History of the British Army.* Good Lord! Who'd have thought it had so much history? I pulled out Volume Thirteen, figuring that should be about the Great War, but it wasn't. It covered the Crimea and some stuff I'd scarcely heard of. Glancing at the title page, I saw it was by a chap named Fortescue and was printed in 1930 in Toronto, Canada, of all strange places. Well, if this was a sample, I couldn't see myself raiding my employer's shelves for bedtime reading.

My immediate duties done, I sat down in my room and started to think. Maybe I should spend this spare time writing. I got out things to write with. After sitting blankly for a while, I decided that, as I could not think of anything at all to write, I would make a line on the page. Someone at the club had told me that painters do that, when they can't get started.

I don't know whether it would have worked for me because as soon as I'd made the mark on the page I heard the suite door open, so I left my opus and went to be a valet again.

I found the Honourable Frederick putting his things away where they belonged without waiting for my assistance. Apparently, he was used to there being no one there to help him. From the way he moved, I thought at first that he might be a little the worse from drink but decided no, he was just depressed and tired.

"Well, Rodney Anson Goodale, she liked the tie. She said that for once I had got it right. That was a good start, but the next part was what we highbrow fellers call The Bird.

"It turns out she likes men who Do Things: you know, climb mountains, explore jungles, paint pictures, write books, run for parliament, all that sort of stuff. Any thoughts, Goodale?"

"I would consider it a liberty to give any opinion, sir."

"Nonsense. Well, you don't really know enough at present. Theorizing without data, Sherlock Holmes would say and be right, as usual."

Aha! I thought. He doesn't read just dusty old histories.

"Well, sir, if you get some sleep, perhaps things may look better in the morning."

He wandered over as if to get a drink. I expected him to pick up my note, as he must have seen I'd left one, but he stopped and turned, like a Guardsman on parade.

"My horse?"

"She won by a short head, sir."

He clapped his hands together and decided he did not need alcohol to buck him up, as a victory on the turf had done that. Now he could face bed.

"Good night, Goodale."

"What time do you like to rise, sir?"

"Hell, whenever I get up, I'll tell you I'm up. Just you go to bed and be ready for me tomorrow."

CHAPTER
— 5 —

SOME CLAIM TO FIND IT DIFFICULT TO SLEEP IN A strange place. I slept like a newborn and was already up and dressed and in the kitchen when I could hear my employer moving about. I lit the gas to boil his eggs. I had laid out clothes for him, but with no idea what he intended to do, I could just hope they were appropriate.

I sliced the bread, put it into the toaster, and folded up the sides. It was not a model with which I was familiar, so I took care to check before I thought it would be brown, and just as well: it was already burnt on the one side. I turned the slices over and folded it up again but not for so long. I ate the burnt toast myself to destroy the evidence.

"I smell burnt toast," the Honourable Frederick greeted me. "Don't throw it out. I'll eat it. I don't want to waste money."

"It's all right, sir," I assured him. "I like my toast a bit overdone, so it did not go to waste."

"No? Well, let's have the eggs, and if they're hardboiled, that's just too bad, too."

"They should be as you wanted them, sir," I said, hopeful but without a firm belief in my own statement of assurance.

I put the first one in the egg cup, and he smashed in the top.

"Oh, yes: perfect. You're hired."

"Thank you, sir," I replied.

As long as he keeps hiring me, I thought, I have a job. I shall need to listen carefully, though. Sometime soon he may say "fired" instead of "hired." They do sound similar, and I might not hear him correctly.

I had wondered whether he might continue to speak of the lady of last night. He didn't. At least for the time being he seemed to have put her aside.

I made him tea, and I picked up the dishes to wash. It was at that exact point that like a big lump of mud in the face it hit me that not only had I not written one line, but I had no ideas at all, not anything. Like one of those grim Sahara deserts, my mind was just sand.

Now I was feeling down, and I couldn't even blame it on some woman. Come to think of it, I didn't really know any women. The few in the mob at the pub weren't for me or I for them. That was it: women. If I went about looking for girls to take out, I might get a spark of an idea to start me writing. Also, it wouldn't be long before I had more money to add to the leftover cab fare. Even now I was almost rolling in it. The voice in my head said, "I always win."

While I was washing the breakfast dishes, my employer came into the kitchen, pipe in hand.

"Goodale! I have to go to Whitehall to see an old chum of mine. You mind the shop while I'm out. Order something for lunch or whatever. I have no idea how long this will take."

"Very good, sir. Would you like me to help you into something more formal?"

"Oh, no, not on the cards. It's just an old friend, not an official meeting of some kind. This suit is fine. I'm off."

I felt like responding, "Do write, if you have time," but decided he might not see that as humour. I daresay writing was on my mind more than a bit.

Then he was gone. I finished the dishes, then sat and stared about the room. Presumably I would get used to the Honourable Frederick's habits, if I managed to hold onto the job long enough. If he always spent so much of his time out, I'd have the opportunity to write. Surely there was something in my recent experiences to write about, some starting point. Nope. If it was there, I could not see it. Maybe if I ducked out of the suite instead of phoning in a lunch order, something would happen to me.

I took the menu card down to the main floor, where a person sat at a desk with a little sign that said: "Hotel Services." Well, she wasn't just "a person." She was a small, cute blonde in a becoming dark green hotel service dress. That perked me up a bit.

"Pardon me," I addressed her with, I hoped, a charming smile. "I would like to order lunch for 304. I assume it is you I confer with?"

"That's right. She didn't return my smile.

She did glance at the clock on the side wall: 10:35. Was that too early for lunch? "You're Mr. Oglethorpe's man, aren't you?"

Not wanting her to think I was just a hey-you, I put on the dog a bit.

"Yes, for now I am working as his valet, but I am really a writer."

The words did not have the effect I'd intended. She frowned in distaste.

"Oh. One of those nosey types that dig up the dirt on the well-to-do, eh?"

"No, no," I assured her hastily. "Not at all. A writer of fiction. Novels, you know."

"Don't try to square it now. You're a news-hound. Well, I will warn the staff about you. Lunch doesn't start until eleven."

"I see I can't change your mind," I sighed and gave her my lunch order. I was hungry, but it wouldn't taste as good now, I reflected.

The lift boy was the same as the day before. He must have worked long hours. When I got in to return to 304, I remarked to him, "That woman at the Hotel Services desk is a bit too much, isn't she?"

"Oh, you found that out, did you?" he

chuckled. "Yes, she is—shall I say—a bit daffy. Nice to look at, though."

"She thought I was a newspaper writer."

"Well, if you are, please put me in your story. I never got my name in the papers yet, and I'm nineteen already."

"Well, if I ever do write for a paper, I promise you will be in it."

"Good! My name is Bill Perkins."

"Right," I said.

I wrote it down in my unused notebook and left the lift. Someone wanted it higher up; the bell was ringing.

As the lift doors slammed shut, I realized that after two attempts at literary art, that name was the first thing I had actually written. The struggle and frustration brought back to me my old feelings in school. While my father was at sea, a friend of my mother's told her about a school in Cheltenham that was good and not too expensive, so she decided to send me there.

When I arrived, I didn't think much of the place from any point of view, but I tried to make the best of things. Unfortunately, I got into a bit of a punch-up over a cricket match and was sent to the headmaster.

Without bothering to hear what I had to say, he just got the strap out of a cupboard, grabbed my wrist, and gave me ten. It hurt, of course, but I didn't show it. When he turned to replace the strap, I grabbed his big silver inkpot and dumped ink all over his books and desk. Then I walked back to my room and packed my few things. Although I hadn't much money, I did have enough for train fare home, so I left for the station.

When, late in the day, I arrived home, I found that my father had returned temporarily from wherever he'd most recently been. I decided that a straightforward telling of my story was all I could do, so that's what I did.

He heard me out with a very stern face. Then suddenly he started to laugh. In moments he was roaring with laughter. Upset, my mother objected, but he said some slightly rude Royal Navy things and started laughing again.

Next day he rang up the school to inform them that I was withdrawn. About two weeks after that he fell and broke his right arm, so I had to learn how to shave a person with a cut-throat razor, a recommendation for a valet, although the Honourable Frederick appeared to prefer to shave himself—with a straight razor, not one of the modern things.

Anyway, what had reminded me of my leaving that school was the same feeling of indignant fury the blonde woman at the desk provoked in me by her failure to listen to what I said. This time, however, I could do nothing about it. Oddly enough, there was a very similar inkpot in 304, but somehow that did not seem quite the approach for this occasion.

Soon after eleven my food arrived, and the maid who brought it was most kind and attentive. I suspected she'd heard the story about my being a newsy and wanted to make sure I put her in the paper, too—with her name spelled correctly.

This lunch, sausage and mash, was actually quite good; even the chicken soup, which I've found tends towards the watery, was very tasty. Had the cook heard the newspaper thing? Maybe it wasn't so bad to be wilfully misunderstood after all.

After I ate, I cleared away pipe ash again, and then I got busy assiduously brushing and rehanging the Honourable Frederick's clothes. I seemed to have got over my shyness. I was not prying into someone else's possessions, I reminded myself, but doing the job for which I'd been hired. He had a fair array of garments, all expensive, similar, and dull. "Not my concern," I remarked to no one. If he asked my advice, I'd give it. Otherwise, I'd keep my mouth shut.

His shoes were about the same as his other apparel: nice, expensive, not too up to date. I found the polishing kit under the kitchen sink. After the dumpy school I'd removed myself from, I was sent on to Westgate. There they had a cadet corps, and through their great care I learned how to polish shoes—well, boots, rather, but the idea is the same. What's more, I liked the job; it gives one a sense of doing something really worth doing.

I was hot at that when the master returned to his lands. He had a lot of shoes, and they'd been let go. He bustled in, said thanks, when he saw the shiny footwear, and ignored the bit of mess I'd made and not cleaned up yet.

"I should have asked before: have you got a passport?"

"Yes, sir," I assured him. "I was recently in France."

"Good, good. I lost a couple of valets because I had to sail at once, and they had no papers. I should have made sure the agency knew that, and I forgot. I hadn't expected to be going so soon. Well, all's well that ends well."

"When do we leave, sir, and where do we go?"

"Oh, I'm not sure yet of the time, but we are going to New York City."

I almost jumped up and down for joy. New York City! Where could a writer find better material? Paris is dead, London boring and stale, but New York is vibrant, filled with lights and fun. They even have an ice hockey team. Maybe I could watch a game. I'd never seen one before, but I had read about the sport and watched some news reel clips. It looked really fast. I thought I might even enjoy playing myself, if I could learn to skate.

Lost in my daydream and finishing up with the shoes, I was peripherally aware of the Honourable moving about, getting things out of drawers and so on. Wasn't that part of my job? Well, he seemed not to need help. He brought out a rather worn brown briefcase, such as solicitors use.

"Any use for this," he asked me, "or does it get chucked out with the other rubbish?"

"If you don't mind, sir, I would really appreciate that for the paper I bought a few days ago. I have nothing to put it in."

"Well, it's yours, then. It has my initials on it, but the letters are already well worn, so I don't think that will matter. It will spare me the cost of shipping it, too, " he added, as he set off to get a drink rather than telling me to fetch it.

I did not point out that, if I was going and brought the case with me, it would be on the waybill somewhere or other—stands to reason, I mean.

He settled down with his drink and pipe to read the afternoon paper, while I attended to the small task of packing my trifling holdings. I wanted to be ready to leave as soon as my rather unpredictable employer decided to. First came the quire of typing paper I had purchased, perhaps an eccentric action when I'd had no typewriter, no knowledge of how to use one, and very little money, but things were going better now. Proudly I placed it in my new briefcase and closed it up with an efficient-sounding snap.

Belatedly, I discovered that I had just locked the case and had no key. That had been stupid.

I felt like the chap who is taken in by the three card trick man at a party. My first impulse was to go out and ask my boss if he had a key for the thing, but I hesitated to show myself such a fool.

The lock was little, after all. It would probably open with a hair pin. Of course, in an entirely male establishment like ours, there wouldn't be a hair pin. Hmm. Well, I'd work that out later.

Meanwhile, if I had a story to get down, I had my notebook.

I re-entered the sitting room to see the Honourable Frederick putting on his coat and hat. I hustled over to hand him his cane. What now?

"Just going for a walk," he told me. "Be back soon."

He left. I looked about the room for something to clean up and noticed amid the ashes by his chair a detective story by that American chap Dingwall who lives over here: big-time writer, lots of books and plays on the wireless, even interviews. I'd read a couple of his novels myself and thought they were pretty straightforward. His P. K. Metcalfe was no genius but more a down-to-earth, hardworking detective. I bet that would be easier to write, too. Not a bad thought. Could I write a detective story myself? It wasn't what I'd had in mind, but then I'd so far had nothing in mind and less than nothing on paper.

Beside the Dingwall book lay the newspaper the Honourable had been reading. If he were finished with it, I should clear it away, but was he? Musing, I noticed a clue. Well, it would have been a clue in a story. There was a section cut out of the topmost page.

Thinking like a detective, I noted the date and the edition: yesterday's. Maybe he'd gone out for a more up-to-date one, but he could have bought that here in the hotel.

I put his used glass and some other dishes into the kitchen sink to wash and took the stairs down to the newsstand in the main lobby. There I asked the man if he still had the paper I wanted. He did and was happy to sell it to me rather than turn it back in for the possible refund.

Like a real private eye, I mounted the stairs

to the suite, entered the kitchen, and quietly closed the door behind me. As the afternoon was advancing, I turned on the overhead light before I picked up the newspaper. Oh! I realized; I'd left a step out. I put down my paper again and went out to the one in the sitting room. Without moving it, I checked the page number and the position on the page of the piece, as they call it.

Then I returned to my special investigation parlour and located the part that had been cut out of the other paper. In a section dealing with entertainment—shows and that sort of thing—this was a report on why a popular West-end production Jumped Up Jenny was closing—in fact, had closed. That was interesting. I hadn't seen it, of course, but I'd heard it was quite good: rather a silly plot about a girl who pretends to be something or other in order to win a chap who, it turns out, loves her for what she really is, but lots of good song and dance numbers.

It seemed that some serious disagreements had arisen between the theatre owners and the people behind the theatre company. A recent smash hit in New York, the production had been brought over here and enjoyed a very successful run so far. The problems appeared to have come up over how the loot was to be divided.

So why should Oglethorpe care? Did he have money in the show himself or a general interest in theatre? Possible, but unlikely. Then I noticed at the end of the piece a short interview with a member of the company, a singer and dancer named Elizabeth Weston, along with a small picture of a pretty blonde. A light went on in my head: this must be the lady who'd given the Honourable Frederick the bird. There was no hard evidence, true, but I knew it was so.

Just like a PI story: a nice bit of detective work and a touch of inspiration. Too bad I couldn't use it. In addition to the boot, it might earn me a broken nose as well. It was certainly none of my business, and I should set it aside, but it had been fun while it lasted.

Hearing the door to the suite, I hastily tidied away the evidence. It occurred to me that, whatever my employer's dinner plans, he might like some cocoa before bed. I'd noticed a tin of it in the kitchen cupboard next to the shoe polish.

CHAPTER
— 6 —

As it transpired, there were no dinner plans. He sent me down to the Service Desk to order Boeuf Bourguignon. He said it saved on the telephone, as the hotel charged per call. I must admit I hadn't known that. In fact, I wouldn't have thought of it. Still, I could feel a bit smug at having gone downstairs to order lunch.

The disagreeable beauty was away from the desk, replaced by an older woman who was big on efficiency and small on chat, which was fine with me. When the staff brought up our meal, I settled the Honourable Frederick in the dining room before I went to eat in the kitchen. He acted happy enough, but for a fellow with irregular eating habits for the past few months, I found my first experience of Boeuf Bourguignon, a sort of beef stew, tasty but rather skimpy.

I decided to make cocoa for myself, even if he didn't want any, but when I returned to the living room later to ask him, he said he would, and he seemed pleased I'd thought of it.

In addition he asked, "Are you ready to go, Goodale: packed, I mean?"

"Oh, yes, sir," I was able to assure him. "When do you want me to buy the train tickets?"

"Oh, forget about tickets," he replied with a wave of the pipe in his hand, sprinkling ash on his chair. "I've rented a car to take us to Southampton."

"Very good, sir. When do you wish to leave?"

"No fuss. Sometime tomorrow, I think. I'll work that out. There's lots of time. The Princess Alexandra doesn't sail for a couple of days yet."

"Then should I get in touch with a hotel in Southampton, sir?"

"Oh, I phoned on ahead to The Three Hearts. We shall be well received, but I shall retain these rooms here. I may be back soon. It is a bit uncertain."

I nearly laughed. Saving a penny on the house phone and then renting cars and rooms as if they cost nothing! Still, I withheld the guffaws. I needed the job, and I wanted to see New York City.

Next morning I boiled up all the eggs and toasted a lot of the remaining bread. I'd got quite skilled with the toaster. I took him in what he wanted and ate the rest myself. It therefore would not go to waste, saving sixpence.

After breakfast he handed me a bunch of one-pound notes.

"Here's some money. Take it about to tip the staff who have helped us. Then we shall be well received on our return."

I said nought and marched out to do his bidding. I decided to miss the blonde who had a dislike for me and instead gave one pound to Bill Perkins, the lift attendant. I also gave two pounds to Sammy, the doorman. I might need him later for information on horses, etc.. The balance went to cleaning staff, maids who brought up the food, etc. He would be well remembered—a nice idea, if he could afford it. It was certainly a puzzle. I would suppose he must be well off, but he kept on worrying about pennies. It was beyond me, so I let it go.

Given my employer's intermittent economy, I estimated that we must be overdue for a reaction in that direction. I wasn't expecting a large four-door, flashy-looking sedan to drive up, but it did. Once more I found myself left out. Willing helpers loaded the car with the Honourable Frederick's modest number of cases and trunks, and he made it obvious that he intended to drive this classy machine himself.

"Hoy! Let's roll!" he cried to me in glee from behind the steering wheel.

He'd placed a glossy new briefcase on the front passenger seat, so I got into the back with the luggage to be out of his way. That made him look like my chauffeur, but he didn't mind, so why should I? Off we went, not too fast at first, but once we were clear of London, we saw what this thing could do. My employer had a great time roaring all the way to the Three Hearts Hotel, just on the edge of Southampton. It had a large playing card for a sign. Funny, I'd assumed it would be three harts—deer, you know. I wondered if the proprietor had won the hotel with a hole card that was only a three.

Leaving most of our gear in and on the car, we took with us just what we might need for camping overnight, so to speak. That is, the Honourable did. I had only my one suitcase and my briefcase altogether. I could carry those and one of his as well. I noted that he brought his own briefcase himself.

Once again we had a suite, but a smaller one this time: a sort of central living room with a bedroom off to either side. The master took the larger room, and I set myself up in the other one, a bit cramped but good enough for a short stay and palatial compared to my mousehole at Mrs. Bleary's.

For a wonder, he let me help him unpack and stow away his things, although he did not sit quietly in the living room while I did it but worked beside me, getting in my way. Then he phoned down for food, something French again, a fricassee, insisting that I sit at the table with him.

"I'm lonely today," he explained.

I suppose some servants would have informed him coldly that this was not the properly done thing. Well, he was the boss, and he did look a bit down. Strange. I'd have thought all that racing car stuff he'd pulled on the way would have cheered him up enough. Odd, too, that no one ever asked me to drive, not even, it appeared, if it were my job.

We ate in silence except for a small wireless playing dreamy music, "My Blue Heaven" for one thing, offstage somewhere. I thought I should leave it to him to start the conversation, if he wanted one. He didn't. Shortly after we had eaten, there came a knock on our door. I opened it, and the clerk from the front desk in the lobby handed me the tickets for the liner. Then he left, not expecting a tip from me. In turn, I passed them on to Mr. Oglethorpe, who looked at them as if checking something.

"I could get only a stateroom," he told me. "You can have the extra room, so I'll save not getting you a second-class cabin."

I felt sort of insulted, as if he didn't trust me out of his sight, but I knew that was just silly. In addition to his aversion to wasting money, he would naturally like the staff to be on call. Next door to him, I could have little in the way of excuse not to be available most of the time, whereas a few decks down I might get distracted or lost. Still, I did have that hemmed-in feeling.

Well, it would not interfere with my writing. That had not advanced an inch. I still had nothing to tell the teaming thousands of my waiting public. This is ridiculous, I told myself; there must be something to write about, but when I fell asleep, I hadn't yet had any ideas.

CHAPTER
— 7 —

NEXT MORNING WE WERE OFF TO THE BIG BOAT. Our car took us quickly to the required pier, where we handed over the luggage to some people who would take care of all that for us. I was left standing by the car until a man came with a paper, showed it to me, and collected the keys. I had to sign for this transaction, as the Honourable Frederick had wandered off down by a white picket fence.

When he returned a short time later, he didn't ask what had happened to the car. He simply collected me, and we went on board the RMS Princess Alexandra. It was huge. Most of the upper works were white, and the two funnels were black, but for colour there were lots of flags flying. Many sailors, very neatly dressed in blue jackets and white hats with the ship's name, ran about looking like they really did know how to make this enormity do things.

One of the ship's personnel—I had no idea yet who anyone was properly called or what they did—took us up to a high level he referred to as the Promenade Deck and ushered us into a stateroom with a big room to the left and a small one to the right. Mister Oglethorpe pointed to the latter, and I took in my meagre luggage. There wasn't much open space, but the bed was nice, and there were lots of places to put clothes and things. Stowing them, my old man would have called it.

The central room was much bigger and had a lot of large, rather modern furniture and a bar, all of it built in or fastened down. I went on through to the main bedroom, where the master had opened a trunk and was staring into it. Firmly, I edged him away and went about unpacking for him. This time he stopped messing about and even seemed grateful to be able to let me get on with my job. That chap never did seem to have any notion of the correct procedure in these matters. I admit that this was my first run at serving as a valet, but I had heard chaps talk about it and read books that give you the general idea. Why did he not seem to get it?

Once I'd finished unpacking as much as he thought he'd need, I summoned a person called, I think, a steward to remove the empty cases and any "not needed on the voyage," as they seemed to call it, a neat phrase, I thought, if a bit sinister-sounding. My boss insisted on keeping a trunk I'd wanted to send away, but I really felt quite competent.

The Honourable instructed me to order up a good array of various sorts of drinks. That involved a different steward, as it turned out, one I never saw again. Anyway, I accomplished my mission to my employer's satisfaction. I assumed we would be entertaining someone, or more than one, and hoped my ability to mix drinks would be up to the challenge.

Mr. Oglethorpe grabbed me by the shoulder and said, "Now we need a signal. If I want this suite to myself, I shall raise one finger: thus," he illustrated, as if he were a teacher displaying the number one to a dunce class.

"I see, sir," I nodded. "Then I go out, but when do I come back?"

"That's easy," he said, releasing me: "use the telephone. If I answer, you can come back. If not, stay away. There's lots to do on these big boats. Go look."

Obediently, I took a walk about the Promenade Deck. It was beautifully decorated in woods of various colours and lots of really interesting art work. I saw lounges, withdrawing rooms, shops, bars, various dining places, all lovely and carefully planned. Even better, we seemed to have on board quite an array of feminine beauty. I would be remiss not to grasp this opportunity to increase my knowledge of women. Perhaps I'd fall in love; that would give me something to write about. At least it had worked for Shakespeare.

Further following the suggestion of the master, I extended my walk to other parts of the ship. I wondered how the second and third class passengers lived. I found stairs to descend and was proceeding towards the bow on the main deck when I heard repeated hoots of a big horn and the clang of a ship's bells. Like a huge creature stirring from sleep, the Princess Alexandra shook and shimmied and then very slowly commenced to move. The sun was now high and the cloudless sky a vivid blue. Little tugboats hauled and nudged the immense craft to get her pointed in the right direction. I must admit it was all very exciting. I couldn't see why everyone wasn't out watching this display of the seamanship that had made Britain great.

When I reached the bow, I joined the few other people who found this interesting. All of them were men, I noticed. The spray came right over us. As I could not get wetter, I stayed there for a while, and I began to understand what my father found in the Navy.

All my life he had been going off on some sort of job. When he came back, he was always beefing and grumbling about how tough things were, with no hope of advancement or decent money, and all the things he had to buy out of this own pocket. The complaints flowed on endlessly. I found it easy not to notice that he had been promoted, and that he did make more money. He didn't harp on those things. No matter what level he reached, he had lots of negative things to say about the sea service.

So it was no wonder at all that I'd had no desire to become a naval officer. I did not want to go to the naval academy, and I didn't. My father was totally stunned at what he saw as my strange attitude. It was inexplicable. At least my little brother Dickie liked railroads and airplanes. Writers were lavender-spatted poseurs or grubby, drunken newsies. I must admit that he did not press me on this. Instead, he assumed that, given time, I would wake up and see the light.

This was not it. Perhaps the very strength of his conviction worked to strengthen my resistance. I did, however, begin to form a more balanced view of things than I had got from what he said and the few times my mother had taken us to the smelly docks to watch his ship pull out of harbour.

After a while I remembered that I had set out to see what second and third class were like and resumed my prowl. If not as luxurious as first class, second class was surprisingly impressive. I decided to see what second-class saloons were like. The cost per drink was probably the same, but I wanted to get some idea of the atmosphere among the slightly less well-to-do, sailing for business or pleasure, what they said and felt.

Spotting an establishment with the look of an Olde English village pub, complete with leaded glass windows and yellow lights, I walked in and looked about. I was disoriented to find myself surrounded by mostly women, mostly attractive young women, in fact, all talking at once and all talking with American accents. So much for Olde England. Then it hit me that this must be the returning theatre company that the Honourable Frederick was interested in. That was why we were all of a sudden heading for New York—not that I minded in the least. I was looking forward to it. Before walking into a room full of lovely women, however, I would have liked to change into dry clothes. If I was no longer exactly dripping from the spray, I was still pretty moist.

Without difficulty I recognized Elizabeth Weston from the little picture in the newspaper. She was sitting at a table with some other people. Her picture hadn't lied; she was a very good-looking lady. She wore her shoulder-length golden hair fluffed up around her face to frame her perfect features. Her china-blue eyes shone against her white skin. Oh, she was a looker all right, no mistake. She was definitely from the States; she had to speak loudly to carry over the general babble, so, although I couldn't follow her conversation, I did hear her voice.

I guess I must have been staring. She looked right at me. Did she notice I was damp and wonder why? Was she trying to place me in this troop? Her gaze was embarrassing. I went up to the bar and ordered a gin and tonic. Then I wandered about, enjoying the scenery. These women were chosen at least partly for their looks, and they lived up to it.

I thought I should report this news item to the boss. Then I realized that I needed to exercise some tact, or I'd displease him in a big way. He had not told me anything about this lady, or, indeed, these people. If I wished to keep my job, I had better act dumb.

The troop was so lively and enthusiastic that I just stood there for a few minutes, leaning against the wall and basking in it as I sipped my drink. Their London tour had ended more quickly than it should have, but they were probably a little homesick by now and ready to enjoy the return journey. Funny. I'd always thought of New York as a place you go to, not one you come from: silly, but true.

The Weston lady was turned toward one of her friends. I took a good look at her as I edged out of the pretend pub. The Honourable Frederick had excellent taste. I found the companionway and descended another set of stairs to the third-class cabins: again, not at all bad; very comfortable, in fact. No squalor here.

After a bit of a look around I went up on deck, sat down on a bench facing the rolling sea, and took out my notebook and pencil. Without hesitation I started to write about what I had seen and felt among all those show people. At last I was a writer in more than fantasy! If it wasn't what I'd intended to write, well, I felt exhilarated to be writing anything at all.

Then I realized with a start that I had been away from home, so to speak, for quite a while. Granted, my employer had told me to have a look around, but had he quite grasped the size of the ship and the huge area inside it?

I had to climb up a lot of stairs because I could not find a lift. (There was one. I found it later.)

When I made it back to the stateroom, I went in with some trepidation. The Honourable was there, feet up and drink in one hand and pipe in the other.

"Well," he greeted me with a smile, "you had a stroll around?"

I was relieved he seemed in a good mood.

"Yes, sir. This thing is huge."

"True. I haven't sailed on her before, but I did read a bit about her. Anyway, when you were going about the ship, did you happen on any Americans?"

So that was how we were going to handle things. Very well.

"Oh, yes, sir," I admitted. "I'd expect there'd be lots of them going home."

"True," he agreed and then got to the point more quickly than I'd thought he would, "but I am thinking of a theatre company from New York who were in London but are supposed to be returning home on this vessel."

"Now that you mention it, sir, yes, there was quite a crowd of Americans, mostly women, in a pretend English pub in second class."

"You mean they are not travelling first class?"

he said in a sort of shocked horror.

"If this was them, sir, then, no, they were definitely in second class, and it's a fair way down."

"Do you think they still might be there?"

"Could be, sir. They seemed in no hurry to leave."

"Great. Then lead me to this pub in the second class."

My sense of direction wasn't too great yet, so we ended up going a long way around. The Princess Alexandra must have been coming into open sea. She had started to roll a bit, which made walking more difficult. I began to worry about delivering my employer to the right place in time.

In the end, however, I did find the pub, and there were lots of people in it still, so I couldn't be faulted. Although I was careful not to focus on her in particular, Elizabeth Weston was still at the same table, large as life.

The Honourable Frederick advanced upon her, waving in an off-hand but friendly manner. Her gaze lit on him and then briefly travelled to me before returning. Oh, yes, she remembered me.

"Well, Elizabeth!" he exclaimed. "Whatever are you doing here?"

"Oh, didn't you hear?" she countered with the convincing innocence of an actress. "They closed the show and are shipping us back to where we came from."

Now that I saw the woman again, she was even better looking than I'd remembered, and I got a closer view as she stood up and reached for a short green jacket. She was wearing a flowered pink dress that clung to her graceful figure and failed to hide much of her shapely legs. Someone had once told me that dancers had legs like cart horses, but she certainly didn't. Maybe she hadn't been doing it long enough.

The Honourable Frederick was there in a flash, helping her on with her jacket and holding her green handbag while she got herself sorted out.

"Won't you let me buy you a drink?" he offered.

"No, thank you, Freddie," she smiled. "Maybe another time. I was just on the way to my cabin."

"What about luncheon then?" he urged.

This was getting embarrassing. I walked out the

door. If he wanted me and I'd disappeared, he'd be annoyed, but he'd be worse than annoyed if I hung about when he didn't want me. Flustered, I all but collided with a small, dark girl with freckles who appeared to be about to enter the pub.

"Oh, I am sorry! I do beg your pardon!" I told her, taking her arm to steady her.

"No harm done," she assured me and started to turn away.

Just to say something as a sort of greeting to open a conversation, I asked her the way to the third class. Without speaking, she pointed toward the clearly marked stairs.

I said, "Thank you," and we parted company. I think this is what they call a strike-out in baseball. I'd never had the opportunity to watch an entire game, but I had seen at the pics some bits of famous players and big moments in the sport. Funny. People say it's like cricket, but it didn't seem that way to me at all. Maybe I'd soon get the chance to learn more about the game and form a better-grounded opinion.

Cheered, I proceeded on my way. I knew already where the third class was, of course, so I just trickled down the stairs. Last time there I hadn't looked around much. I'd been too busy starting my career as a great writer and then worrying about endangering my current job as a valet. I thought I should find out more about it than that the area seemed clean and fairly comfortable. Also, I wanted to give the Honourable Frederick time to carry out his plans regarding the Weston lady. In an hour or so I'd find a telephone and ring him up. Meanwhile, I advanced into the uncharted territory. I don't suppose my dad's maps, or charts, would still call it Terra Incognita. I'd seen that on old maps at school and thought it sounded like a lady continental film star.

I found a pub with music playing, just records, no dance bands here. I recognized "My Blue Heaven," always an old favourite. The décor was functional, modern, and slightly cold looking, with square-built, light-coloured wooden furniture, the stools at the bar similar to the chairs at the tables but higher. Everything looked well-scrubbed but somehow a trifle uninviting.

Nonetheless, there was a moderate-sized crowd, much more mixed in appearance than the theatre company in second class. I wandered over to the bar and sat down not too far from a nice-looking young woman of about my own age, say between twenty and twenty-two. She had dark brown bobbed hair and wore a tailored blue dress that hugged a remarkably fine figure.

Sitting down was all very well, but I couldn't think of a thing to say to her. What had seemed "not too far" was about seven feet away, and I would have to project my opening remarks over the recording of some American lady blues singer with remarkably good lungs who had followed "My Blue Heaven." Discouraged, I ordered a gin and tonic from the barman and sat trying to look interesting and important—well, something other than still damp.

When the woman turned her head to glance past me, I got a better view of her face. Despite rather dark, rich, creamy skin, she appeared to have blue eyes, a stunning combination. A charm bracelet on her left wrist seemed to jingle on its own every so often. If she was aware of me, she certainly gave no sign of it. Experience with women turned out to be hard to get.

As a change, I welcomed a cute, friendly girl who came by selling cigarettes, and I bought a pack of American Lucky Strikes. I'd never tried them before, but I hoped it would prove a good omen. You know: there I was, thinking about baseball and strike-outs, and now this. Hmm. Well, maybe.

Nonchalantly, I picked up a tiny box of free ship's matches and lit one of my cigarettes. I had never, in fact, smoked any American cigarette before, and I didn't know what to expect. They have some horrible cheap smokes in France. In comparison, these were rather good, but the fair lady down the bar continued not to notice. Oh, well.

I gave up. I took out my notebook and started to record what had happened since I'd boarded the Princess Alexandra. The more I wrote, the easier it became. I realized that I might have a newsworthy bit on the New York theatre people. I had come to a description of Elizabeth Weston, when I felt a sort of shadow over me. Startled, I glanced around. Golly! It was the lady I'd been looking at and given up on. She was quite tall. Yes, her eyes were blue, a sort of sea blue, extraordinarily fetching.

"Are you a writer?" she asked.

"Well, yes," I admitted, "I have been writing

for a while." Say, about ten minutes, I failed to add.

"Do you write about politics and labour?"

Did I?

"Well, I just did a piece on the New York theatre company that lost its run in London due to a dispute about funds received. I suppose that's labour."

She frowned and shook her head.

"No, I mean coal miners and lorry drivers: that sort of labour."

Was this a more attractive version of the women back in my London local? What would she like to hear that wouldn't be a totally unsupportable lie?

"Well, no, but I have been giving a lot of thought to the problems of the Royal Navy."

"No, no, that's not it. I mean social concerns, the struggle of the helpless workers in a merciless capitalistic society that callously flattens them like beetles."

She really did have the most seductive eyes. With them riveted on my face, I found it difficult to worry about beetles, but I had to say something.

"Well, er, I meant to do a small piece on household help."

She made a dismissive gesture.

"That's just for the rich."

"The valets and chambermaids certainly aren't rich," I objected. "Did you know a valet makes only five shillings a week?"

"That much?" she cried. "In addition to room and board? Why, some poor families are forced to manage on half that."

"It's hard to see how they could. A terrible shame, I mean, isn't it? May I buy you a drink?"

"Well, perhaps just one, Mister?"

"Goodale. Just call me Rodney."

"Very well, Rodney. It's so refreshing to be able to talk to someone about the things that really matter. Our society is teeming with frivolity and superficiality. I'm Molly."

She let me buy her a sherry and sipped it but declined a cigarette.

To keep the conversation alive, I ventured, "I was planning an article on lift operators and was just starting a series of interviews with one of them at the Hotel Clarion, when we all of a sudden left on this trip."

"Which operator did you talk to?"

"I remember his name was Bill Perkins. Seemed a nice chap."

"He's my brother. My name's Perkins."

Blimey! What were the odds? Quickly, I tried to think over what I'd told her. Not much, really, thank goodness. Her brother knew I was a valet, but he thought I was a writer, maybe a reporter, which squared with what Molly thought. I'd just have to break the valet news in such a way as not to put her off.

"I haven't known Bill very long," I explained, starting out onto the thin ice. "We met when I took a position as a gentleman's personal gentleman, as they say, with the Honourable Frederick Oglethorpe. Then he decided to travel to New York, so here I am."

"You mean you're doing it for a story?"

I looked sly.

"I wouldn't like to say that."

That was true, at least.

"Then you must be in second class."

Oh, dear. Well, no doubt she could find out, so I'd better tell the truth.

"First, actually," I corrected. "He could only

get a stateroom."

"Then you're not supposed to be down here," Molly frowned.

"No?" I asked, genuinely surprised. "Why not? I was just looking around."

"It's in the brochure."

"Oh. Is there a brochure? I guess the Honourable Frederick has it. Maybe he didn't read it either. He was just down in second class."

Molly sighed.

"Another relic of the obsolete class system. The guidelines aren't enforced much. The underlying assumption is that the first-class passengers won't want to go below their class, and the seconds and thirds will be afraid, or at least uncomfortable, to go above theirs."

"You seem to know a lot about it," I remarked.

At least we were easing away from the struggles of the masses, I thought.

"I have to. I'm a tabby, a stewardess. You know: cleaning, making beds, that sort of thing."

I suddenly knew how the Honourable Frederick had felt.

"In third class?" I cried in dismay.

"That's right," she said defiantly. "Why not?

Those passengers have a right to a pleasant trip, too, you know. They've paid their fare, and a lot harder for them to do it than the fat cats licking the cream up in first."

"Oh, yes, quite," I assured her hastily. "It's just that with your intelligence and seriousness of purpose, you can't be satisfied with such limited opportunities."

I thought that sounded about right. I even meant it. Despite her extreme views, Molly was no guttersnipe.

"Why do you always talk so posh?" she abruptly demanded. "You don't sound like a valet."

Oh, my gosh, another pitfall. I couldn't very well explain that, although I'd learned to talk like her, it was posh that came naturally. Once again, I should stick to as much of the truth as possible.

"I can't stop. My employer can't tolerate harsher speech. If I drop this, I might forget later and receive the Order of the Boot. The agency told me that he'd already let some go on those grounds. I say, I'm not sorry I didn't read the bally brochure. I would have missed meeting you."

She cast down her fathomless eyes.

"But we can't keep on meeting, don't you see? I might lose my job."

I shrugged.

"Why? If we're called on it, which seems unlikely, just say I lied to you, and you thought I was in third class. Can I buy you lunch?"

"Oh, heavens!" she exclaimed, leaping to her feet. "I've overstayed my lunch break already! I'm supposed to be straightening rooms while the passengers eat."

I opened my mouth, but she'd gone.

Well, I thought I had made a start with this girl, but I had not had any vast experience with women, and I certainly had not met any before like Molly. Those at the club sometimes expressed similar views but not with her energy and determination, and not while conscientiously pursuing menial labour themselves. Magnetic: that was it. Molly was magnetic. And forceful.

It was my writing that had attracted her. Well, at least I had made a start with that, too, so I wasn't a complete fraud. Still, I needed some time for cogitation, if I was to have any chance at all, and if I wasn't supposed to be in third class,

I'd better not stay too long.

Also, my employer might very well be wondering where I had got to. I rather hoped he was, anyway. I could use some dry clothes. I found a telephone—free, I noted—and had a call put through to the stateroom. Telephones were something limited to first class.

The Honourable Frederick picked up the telephone and said, "Come home, Aunt Sally."

I replied, "At once, sir," and started on the march back to base.

I had the lady's name and what she did, so I could find her again. So far she seemed reasonably friendly, so I had some cause for optimism. It might be a good time to make friends with our own cabin steward, whom I had seen but not spoken to.

I got back in record time to an atmosphere of gloom. As I entered, there was nothing bright or happy about the Honourable Frederick. I made an effort to think of him so formally because what I'd told Molly about speech actually held true here. If I used any other name, even to myself only, I might make a fatal slip and call him out loud "Freddie, old chum," or something equally disrespectful. Despite his greying hair, he wasn't enough older than I was to claim automatic respect on that account.

He looked down, if not out, as he toyed with an unlit pipe.

"Don't ask," he said, as it I'd have had the effrontery. Perhaps he had once had a valet who'd greeted him on his return home from a date with, "So how'd it go with the bit of fluff, cocky?" but I doubted it. "No," he continued, "I did not get very far with her, but she did say not to call her Elizabeth, as her real pals call her Betsy, so I may have reached the first plateau of a relationship as a real pal."

"I regret I have done nothing to assist you, sir."

I really did feel sorry for him. Despite his flashes of economy, the man seemed to be able to have anything he wanted, except for the one thing that truly mattered to him. It must have festered.

"Oh," he replied, forcing a smile, "I don't see how you can help. If I do, I shall certainly inform you. When you came in, I was just remembering a man we had working for us on the home farm when I was a lad. He was an American. He called himself a hillbilly. Very good with animals and a hard worker. The ladies whispered behind their hands that he'd had to flee the States because he'd killed the man who'd stolen his sweetheart. Maybe so. He did sing some sad songs to himself." He took out some money and handed it to me. "They put me at the captain's table, I see, but I don't feel up to the honour. I'll find some dinner for myself somewhere. You do what you want."

It was ten bob, very generous. I thanked him. He waved his hand and walked out.

First, I changed into drier clothes—my best, because, while it was early for dinner, by the time I needed to be ready, my employer might have wanted me out of the way. I'd probably been assigned a table, too. I should find out about that, but I hesitated to push the button for the steward. Thinking about dinner made me realize I'd missed lunch and was hungry. Altogether, I felt restless and indecisive, so I took a further stroll about first class. I set out in the opposite direction this time to my last exploration and quickly came across a Writing Room, complete with a typewriter—well, three of them actually—and ship's stationery, too, as well as drawers full of postcards of the ship and odd-ments such as pencils, pens, ink, scissors, and tape.

Without hesitation for thought, I sat down, rolled in a sheet of stationery, and started typing. It couldn't be all that hard, after all. Young girls in offices do it, don't they?

Nonetheless, it turned out to be harder physical work than I'd expected. You do have to strike the keys with a certain amount of force. Otherwise, they rise partway and tangle them-selves with the next key you want to press. The keyboard is not in alphabetical order, so you have to search for each key. At first I couldn't figure out how to produce capital letters. A cock-roach might have bettered my first efforts. When our steward appeared, I felt ready for a break.

He was a short chap, rather round although not fat, darkish, with thin, very short hair, a baby face, and large, protruding brown eyes. He wore a white coat with brass buttons and dark blue pants and a worried expression that proved to be habitual.

"Do you know how to work these things?" I asked him.

"No, sir, I'm afraid not."

He had a faint accent I couldn't place.

"Someone must."

"As you say, sir."

Amiable, but not helpful.

"Do you know what I'm supposed to do about dinner? My boss must have been told, I guess, but he didn't pass on the information."

"Oh, yes, sir. It's all in the brochure. Appear at the dining room in forty-five minutes, and someone will direct you to your table. There are usually two or three for passengers travelling first class with their employers."

"I see."

I did see, too. I saw that proper servants would spot me for a fraud in two seconds flat. Even if they didn't, the possibility would not conduce toward an enjoyable meal.

"Where else can I eat dinner?"

"Well, sir, you can order it delivered to your cabin, or you can try the Grill Room, or—"

"The Grill Room: that sounds nice."

"Yes, sir, very nice indeed, the most luxurious dining on the ship. Very superior. When dinner service is concluded, there is dancing as well."

"Where would a stewardess working in third class be right now?"

"A tabby?" he frowned. "Hard to say, sir. Pretty busy. In addition to the cleaning, someone has always neglected to pack a hairbrush or needs assistance to fasten a dress. May I say—"

"That I'm not supposed to leave this class? Yes, she told me. It's in the brochure."

"Yes, sir. Well, then . . ."

"Now look, old boy," I appealed to him, "let's be reasonable. Your name is?"

"Winterhaiter, sir."

"Really? My goodness. Well, mine is Goodale. I'm not a secretary or a paid companion or a nursemaid. I'm just a valet, so you can stop sirring me."

"But you're in first class, sir," he objected.

"True, because my boss could only get a suite. The way you talked about the tables, there must be several of us helper types up here, maybe even other valets. I assume they don't get to sit with the captain, and neither will I."

"True enough, Mr. Goodale."

"Just Goodale is fine with me."

"Me, too," he chuckled, cheering up a bit.

"What a jolly name to have."

"Thanks. Well, here's a bob. I want you—when you can—to take a note down to Molly Perkins in third class. I'd like her to have supper with me in the Grill Room when she gets off duty. Can you do that, Winterhaiter?"

"Well," he reasoned, "it's not actually against the ship's regulations. I mean, even the captain eats with the passengers, but this is sort of different, isn't it? She may not want to chance it."

"True, but let's leave that up to her. I'll write it out now and leave it in your hands."

Not trying for any fancy touches, I didn't have to keep him waiting long. Off he went, and I returned my attention to the typewriting machines. I didn't know how long it would take my messenger to bring me back word. It would be best if I stayed where he could easily find me.

Meanwhile, these contraptions seemed to be challenging me to have another go. I stared at the keyboard and then tried to picture it in my mind with my eyes closed. That didn't seem to help a lot. Next I thought back to people I'd seen typing. Some of them used one or two fingers to pick out the right keys, as I'd been trying to do, and often managed very well. Most of the faster ones, however, held their hands over the middle of the keyboard and moved just their fingers, at least until they had to push the lever at the side to start a new line. I tried that, and it did work rather better. I still had to hunt about for the correct letters, but I could understand how, with enough practice, my fingers might get used to working on their own, like they do when you play a musical instrument.

To start to get the practice I needed, I decided to type one page of my notes on the ship's stationery. That would make it look like a letter, but it would be typed, and this was the paper near at hand. Now I remembered the proper typing paper I'd bought and put into my briefcase and locked away. I had yet to ask about a key or try to open it without one, maybe with a bit of wire.

I set that problem aside for the moment and concentrated on the project before me. It did not go quickly, and I had to X out a couple of words, but it did get done. Now I could refer to my typed notes.

Still no reply from the lady. Well, Winterhaiter could easily find me in my quarters. I went back.

The Honourable Frederick hadn't returned. I picked up his newspaper to read and then had an idea: I could write a story like one of those thrillers I used to love reading at school—not in class, of course. I envisioned a smallish, rat-faced chap as a sort of ingenious master criminal. I'd need to put together a select group of his assistants, and, of course, there was the hero and his sidekick. Really, I would have liked to write a cowboy story, but I didn't know enough about it. I had never even ridden a horse. Horses did not seem to play much of a part in the Royal Navy.

Back to what I was more familiar with. I was thinking in terms of a scene in London when it jarred on me that here I was on a ship that many people would never get to travel on. A maritime plot was beginning to take shape when there was a knock on the door. I opened it to Winterhaiter, who handed me a note.

"Thank you, Winterhaiter, old chap."

I unfolded the paper. She would be happy to join me for supper in the first-class Grill Room and would meet me outside the door at 8:30 this evening.

The steward was still there.

"Sorry it took so long. I think the lady had to give it some thought, but she said she would chance it."

"I shall make sure she has no problems of an official nature," I assured him.

He faded out. I had already donned my best—well, my only—suit when thinking in terms of the dining room. I changed my blue tie for a red one to keep up with the lady's militant attitudes. Then I buffed my already-polished shoes and massed all my funds. My real terror was that I might not be able to cover the prices at this place. Although I had more money than I'd had for months, my fortune might still not be able to stand up to the battering it was likely to sustain this evening. How could I encourage her to go light on the drinks? That would help.

I put my coins in my suitcoat pocket, and just before I left our suite, I borrowed a tiny drop of the Honourable's hair oil. Surely he wouldn't mind, especially if he didn't know. Then I took a deep breath and walked over to the Grill Room. It was early, but not only was I impatient, I didn't want her arriving before me and tapping her shoe at being made to stand alone.

Well, I did get there first. Through the open doors I could see tiers of glittering chandeliers and masses of elegant furniture. There was a band playing, not dance music yet, just a quiet background suitable for dining. Among other tunes I recognized "Love Me or Leave Me." There were lots of people already seated at tables. I was glad to see that most of the men weren't too differently dressed from me, but what if I were expected to have made reservations? I hadn't thought of that.

As if in answer to my concern, a couple passed me, and the man addressed the official at the door: "I hope you can squeeze us in. We didn't book."

He bowed at them.

"You are in luck, sir. As this is the first night at sea, most of the passengers who are good sailors have started in the dining room."

Oh. I hadn't considered that people might not feel hungry, shall we say. I hadn't felt ill crossing the channel, and I didn't now. I reflected briefly how uncomfortable it must be for the ship's officers my father had spoken of who did suffer from seasickness. I'd have considered that reason enough to find another line of work, sort of like a surgeon who couldn't bear the sight of blood.

After about half an hour Molly appeared. I'd begun to fear that she'd changed her mind, but in fairness, she was only five minutes late, and I could see why; she seemed a bit unsteady on her very high heels, a good reason for extending her my arm. Her black shoes, hat, and bag set off her bright red dress and short red jacket. She wore a gold locket thing around her neck, and she looked pretty—no, lovely.

"Good evening, Miss Perkins," I greeted her suavely.

Molly coloured slightly, deepening the lustre of her skin.

"Oh, please, let's not be so formal. We are just two working-class people, out for the evening. Do let's go in."

I asked the official-looking bloke at the door with the made-up tie for a table not too near the band. It sounded good, anyway. He snapped his fingers, and a young waiter type led us to a table tucked away in a corner. We could still hear the band, but since it wasn't time yet for dancing, it wasn't loud.

We sat down and glanced about.

"I've never been here before," Molly volunteered.

"Me neither," I smiled. "Rather a jolly place, what?"

I thought she winced a bit, not a good start.

"A lot fancier than ours downstairs."

"I daresay, but it's the quality of the food that counts, isn't it?"

She picked up the wine list and looked at it. So did I. I was rather holding my breath. Then she put the list down.

"No, I had better not have any. I'd just like something to eat."

My heart leapt up, like the old chap in the poem when he saw a rainbow, or was it a daffodil?

I'm pretty certain it was a poem. Anyway.

"Did you do any writing?" Molly asked.

"Yes, I did," I was glad to be able to inform her, "and I started to type it up. Nowadays, editors prefer typewritten submissions, you know."

"No, I didn't know, but now that you mention it, I can see why they would. Some of the awful handwriting I've seen."

I hoped she wasn't referring to my handwritten

note. I'd thought it would have seemed more personal, but legibility comes first, right? I also hadn't wanted to waste time struggling with the typewriter; I might not have been finished yet. I'd discovered that there was something about the look of the typed page that makes me want to rephrase things.

The Grill Room was very glittery but so carefully lit as to be just bright enough. There were masses of beautiful dishes and cutlery. What a lot of work they'd take to wash and polish, doubtless by people working behind the scenes who wouldn't even get tips unless they divvied them. Maybe there were machines to do the washing, but even so, the tables wouldn't clear themselves into the machines, would they? I reflected that Molly's views might be rubbing off on me.

We both ate rather lightly: the creamed mushrooms on toast. Although she may have thought it daintier not to eat a lot, I suspect she was trying to save me money. I knew I was, but also I was not certain my meal would stay down, if the sea got rougher. The food tasted good anyway.

My lady seemed to watch which fork, etc., I used. At first I thought she was seeing if I used the right one. Then I realized that she was unsure herself. Her hesitant, rather awkward table manners were endearing in comparison with her militant views.

I was also rather touched by Molly's care for my finances. That was a big Plus One for a start. Yes, she was a good-looking, well-dressed lady, but that's only the beginning. The next step is to find out what kind of person she is. I supposed she was doing the same thing.

I thought she'd be saying to herself: I guess he's not a bad chap, and he really seems to like me, but he has very little money at present and scant hope of making a lot more later. Still, she did stay to chat, and she laughed at some of the stories I told her of the artists and writers I'd met in London. I also mentioned my sojourn in Paris without going into a lot of tedious—and unimpressive—detail.

Then I realized I was missing a trick. The band was livening up.

"Would you like to dance?" I suggested.

"Oh, yes! Let's!"

Well, off we went onto the dance floor. As we faced each other, I tried to gather her into my arms, but she pulled away.

"Wake up," she told me. "This is a foxtrot."

Oh, great. Holding her at arm's length, I did my best, but I kicked her in the ankle once and nearly stepped on her foot. She seemed to bear me no grudge and said nothing, but she didn't have to. I suspected that she herself was finding dancing in those high heels more difficult than she'd expected.

I could claim that I was out of practice. I could say that I was unused to that partner. I'm sure those things didn't help, but the truth was that I had never done much dancing. I knew how to waltz, more or less. It looked like it should come naturally, yet when you got out on the floor with the glittering lights and the turning mirror thing on the ceiling and the other couples gliding past, it was not so natural and easy. Although it was pleasant to hold her at all, that also made me nervous and did not improve my dancing, not that she seemed all that good at it either, shoes or no shoes. Given her background and job, she very likely hadn't got a lot of opportunities to learn to dance.

As the band started on a second tune, she

told me, "I think I'd like to sit down again, if you don't mind."

"Of course, yes," I agreed gladly. "Let's have a drink of something," I suggested, to cover the retreat.

"Well, they have beautiful port wine on the ship, and it's not too dear."

"Good. I shall get us a bottle."

"Oh, no," she objected hurriedly. "Just a couple of glasses, please. Remember: I have to get up early next morning and go back to work. That's the trouble with us Cinderellas. In fact, Mr. Goodale, I am really done in. It's been a tough day, with more than the usual quota of things going wrong—no one's fault, just problems."

"I'm afraid life is rather like that. Although I would like to sit here with you all night, I, too, have had a longish day, and I should get back to make sure my employer is still alive and kicking."

"We can come back another evening some time," Molly said, as if she really liked the idea..

"Yes, jolly good. We shall. I'll have Winterhaiter take you a proper typed note next time."

"Yes, jolly good," she mimicked, but she smiled.

I settled the account, which was not too terrible and gave our waiter a bob tip, which would be rather generous, I supposed. I couldn't do this often, but I could do it. We stepped out of the Grill Room with Molly's hand again on my arm.

Softly she whispered in my ear, "I wish I could take off my shoes."

"Me, too," I admitted.

In fact, although I had accomplished as much as possible with polish, my shoes were uncomfortably close to falling to pieces. I'd have to replace them soon, another expense.

As I glanced down, the movement of something black and white caught my eye.

"Is that a cat?" I queried.

Molly directed her own gaze to where I was looking. She looked at it but shivered a bit and was not pleased.

"Yes," she told me, "that's right. It's not one of the regular ship's cats, though. I heard it sneaked on board at some port, and no one noticed right away. That must have been a couple of weeks ago. No one's been able to catch it, though I doubt if they really tried, either. Who cares? I suppose they keep the mice and rats down."

I looked at the cat's face. He had sat down just barely out of the way of passing people and was washing his paws, bold as brass. "I actually own this ship," he declared in the way cats always have.

"What's his name?" I asked.

"How should I know?" Molly laughed. "I don't think it has a name, at least not on board this ship."

I could tell she wanted to get back to her digs and put her feet up, but I kept looking at the cat. He had a very white face with black fur on top of his head and black ears. In fact, most of him was black, except for his face and four white feet with socks of various lengths.

When he looked up straight at me, I saw his name: "Rowney!"

"What?" Molly exclaimed.

"Rowney. He looks exactly like a watercolourist I know named George Rowney. The eyes and his black hair! It's remarkable!"

"Indeed," she pointed out drily, "you just remarked on it. Well, if you like cats, it definitely is one, though I don't know what kind."

"Oh, he's part, maybe mostly, Persian: the long hair and the shape of the head."

She gave me a surprised look.

"You know about cats?"

It did not seem to impress her favourably.

"Well, yes," I admitted. "I do know a bit. We always had cats at home, and—"I stopped myself in time. "But you'll be wanting your sleep."

I shouldn't tell her that my dad was a Navy captain who had told me about cats on various ships, including his own. It was too soon to let her find out that I was part of the established order she'd like to see swept away. Possibly some women might give me credit for rebelling against my class, but somehow I didn't think Molly would take that view. She wouldn't understand, and any romantic ideas about writers would be killed at once.

She led me to a lift, tucked away where it would be handy for staff with trolleys, but not a temptation to exploring passengers. Then she turned.

"Well, sir," she smiled, "I know it is considered proper and respectful to escort the lady home, but in this case I know where I am going, and

you don't, and you may very well have some difficulty finding your way back. Besides, your boss
may be needing you soon."

"I must say that does seem to meet any objec-
tion I might make. Very well. Thank you for an
enjoyable evening."

"I should be thanking you, and I do. I hope
we meet again soon."

She touched my hand, and I clasped hers.

"Well, right-ho, and a jolly good night," I said.

I leaned forward to kiss her—just on the
cheek—but the lift opened, and a sailor emerged
with some sort of machine part on a dolly. Molly
slipped past him, and the door closed behind
her.

I sighed and turned toward my own quarters.
I considered ringing up, but it didn't seem likely
that the Honourable would have advanced to the
point of entertaining company. More probably
he'd have retired early and would not appreciate the disturbance. I had almost reached our
quarters when I caught sight of the black-and-
white cat moving along to my right rear. When
I turned to look, he vanished the way cats do. I
went the rest of the way and on in.

I was alone. I changed into my working clothes and set about emptying the ashtray, sweeping up pipe ashes, and generally tidying up. Then I buffed shoes and checked jackets for loose buttons. I'd noticed a small sewing kit in our luggage, so I supposed that was part of my job. Luckily, I didn't discover any need for mending, as I had no confidence in my ability to made unnoticeable repairs.

CHAPTER
— 8 —

THE HONOURABLE CAME IN ABOUT AN HOUR after me. He was looking pensive. I took his gloves and cane and put them away properly, while he poured himself a brandy without much soda and downed it in one go.

"Ah," he said, "I needed that."

"No doubt, sir," I agreed.

"Yes. I had almost nothing to drink all evening. I was afraid it might not be a good idea in company with the lady."

"Very sound, sir," I chimed in.

I had not thought of that aspect of things myself, though I suspected Molly had. Girls are like that.

"I was disturbed by something she said."

"Indeed, sir?"

"Yes. She commented on something I was talking about." He'd picked up his pipe and been sort of staring into space, but now he turned fully toward me. "She gave me to understand," he continued, "that she was not fond of dogs and really did not approve of hunting."

"Indeed, sir?"

"Yes, indeed. Can you imagine? I was astounded that she should feel that way. I'd never run into such sentiments in my life, not that I can recall, at least."

"I don't know what to say, sir," I confessed.

"Nor me."

I had never hunted myself and didn't much like the idea, but I knew it must be an integral part of his lifestyle, and boys I'd gone to school with had pointed out that foxes destroy large numbers of farm animals, especially sheep.

"Perhaps under the right conditions, she may change her views, sir," I suggested.

"Yes, by George, that may very well be the case. I suppose there aren't many foxes to hunt in New York City."

"True, sir."

"At any rate, I have a job for you." He'd come in carrying a bag, and now he took out of it a beautiful leather-bound album. "I just bought this at the ship's store."

"Very elegant, sir."

"Yes," he agreed, running his strong fingers over the tooled leather. "Well, here's the point: I want you to paste these press clippings"—he pulled open a drawer and took out an envelope—"into this album. The items are all dated. I want you to put them into the book in order of date. Understand?"

"Yes, sir. Very good, sir."

"I also have a pot of glue, so you can get started at once, though I would suggest you go and put on an apron. The glue does get about a bit."

Dressed as instructed, I sat down at a folding card table and began the task. There were certainly lots of clippings: newspaper articles and photos of the New York theatre company's run of Jumped Up Jenny in London over the last couple of months and a few earlier ones, probably from American papers and magazines. He was meticulous and thorough, but was the cause worth it?

Was he always like this about girls, or, indeed, everything? Was there a chest in the attic of the family estate full of similar scrapbooks? I just did not know this chap well enough, although he seemed to have summed me up rather easily. Smart chap, no doubt, eh, what?

Not hurrying, I worked carefully and neatly, and I did get the job done that evening. I then went and got cocoa for both of us. The Honourable Frederick acted appreciative of my services.

Then we both hit the hay. It had been a very long, eventful day.

According to a big compass on display in the main companionway, the ship was heading southwest. I did not have any idea about where anything was or how to get there. So long as the driver of the ship did know, I could sleep peacefully.

In the morning I got the Honourable Frederick his first cup of tea and ordered up his usual breakfast of eggs and toast. I got by with a coffee for myself. I had an urgent mission to carry out. He'd given me a note to deliver to Miss Weston.

There certainly seemed to be no set hours in this job, but I didn't mind acting as messenger. I wanted to see her again. Perhaps at the beginning of the day she'd appear as a real person. Before she'd been a bit removed from reality for me. Now she'd be a flesh-and-blood lady.

I went down to her cabin, or whatever they called it in second class. The Honourable had told me the number. These were each accommodations for four women. The theatre company didn't over-spend on the comfort of its members.

I found the right door and knocked.

Another lady, somewhat older, answered in a pink dressing gown. She offered to give the note to Miss Weston, but I claimed to have been told to place it into her own hands, so after a few moments' wait, she herself appeared in the doorway.

I don't know what I'd expected, but she was rather a disappointment in a simple light-blue cotton dress with a full skirt and a wide collar. She hadn't put much make-up on, and her hair was a bit tousled. Well, this was what she *really* looked like. I'd wanted to know. It crossed my mind to wonder if my employer had ever seen her like that. Probably not. I don't mean to say she wasn't pretty. She certainly was. She just wasn't magic.

With a bow, I handed her the note. She read it.

"May I take back an answer, Miss?"

"Sure," she smiled, and some of the magic reappeared. "Tell him I'm on for the dinner and dancing, OK?"

"Very good, Miss."

I bowed again and turned to go.

"Just a minute," she said, coming out and closing the door behind her.

"Miss?" I queried in apprehension. I hadn't expected this.

"You're Freddie's butler or something, right?"

"Valet, to be exact, but, yes, Miss."

"OK. Have you worked for him long?"

"No, Miss. I just began a couple of days ago."

I reflected to myself that it certainly seemed longer.

"Oh." She looked disappointed. "So you don't know him that well, then?"

"No, not really, Miss, and may I point out that it would not be proper for me to talk about him?"

"No, no, I see that, but we don't have any

mutual friends, and he strikes me as a bit of an oddball, if you get me. A girl's got to be careful."

"I wish I could help you, Miss," I began.

"Oh, don't go all stuffy," she entreated. "I've got pretty good at reading men fast, but he is very hard to read. You have to admit he's different. Like you, now: I can see you're an OK sort of fella, smart, well-dressed, the sort a girl could depend on, but him, I don't know."

"He does seem to be devoted to you, Miss," I ventured.

"Yeah, so he says, but don't they all? Well, thanks anyway, and if I were you, I'd part my hair on the left. It's your best side."

"Thank you, Miss," I told her, at a loss and feeling more than a bit out of my depth.

I returned with my message. The Honourable Frederick was delighted. I did not report to him the details of our conversation, but, then, he didn't ask. I went into my room and parted my hair on the left, my "best side."

When I rejoined my employer, he was sitting in the most comfortable-looking chair with a pipe in one hand and a booklet in the other, probably the brochure Molly had mentioned.

"Have you had breakfast?" he asked me.

"Not yet, sir."

"Well, get some, and charge it to this state-room. That's the easiest. Do you play tennis?"

"Yes, sir."

"And swim?"

"Yes, sir, but I haven't brought swimming trunks with me."

He waved the brochure.

"This says they can provide them. The pool's salt water. Ever swim in salt water?"

"Yes, sir."

"Rummy, isn't it?"

"Tolerably rummy, yes, sir. Buoyant."

He tossed me the brochure. I caught it.

"They've even got a gymnasium with exercise classes. And all sorts of peculiar deck games. Bridge in the lounge. You play bridge?"

"Yes, sir, a little, but I get confused with the bidding over two."

He gave me a straight look.

"You're not a card shark, are you?"

Surprised, I laughed.

"Good lord, no, sir! Why ever should you think that?"

"Well, you have to admit you're a peculiar sort of valet. Never mind. After breakfast, how about tennis and some bridge?"

"As you wish, sir," I agreed. "I suppose they provide rackets."

They did. The Honourable Frederick hadn't brought his own either. He played well. I lost without trying to. Luckily, I gave him enough of a contest to please him. Then he decided we should swim to cool off. After that came lunch in the beautiful but cavernous dining room.

I hadn't lost my nervousness of eating with the other servants, but meals at the assigned tables were included in the fare, and I had to economize somewhere. I'd expected the seating to be balanced between the sexes and was surprised to find my fellow diners predominantly female, most of them ladies' maids. They were pleased to greet a new man and unsuspiciously accepting.

"Where were you yesterday?" a plump, fortyish redhead asked me.

"Mistrustful of my stomach," I replied ruefully. "It seems nice and smooth today."

Although I'd found the meals for the last couple of days tasty, they had often failed to fill in the corners left by months of slim pickings. The dining room went far to make up for it. Instead of ordering a single dish, you could try half a dozen, in addition to soups, salads, desserts, and savouries, plus a choice of a decent red or white wine. I concentrated on what I recognized: chicken pot pie, roast veal, pork cutlets, and sirloin of beef, and wished I'd had room for more. At first I was nervous of appearing too greedy, but most of my fellow diners kept up with me easily.

I listened more than I talked and picked up some hints about the care of clothes. After the meal, opinion was divided between quoits and attendance on their mistresses. One of the two other men was a secretary and above consorting with me. The only other valet was an American who wanted to teach me to shoot craps. When I explained that my employer expected my services, he went off to find someone else.

All in all, we didn't get to the bridge game until afternoon, when we joined a group in the lounge, some of whom appeared to have been playing since breakfast. I'd run into that before: bridge addicts hard at it at the same table day after day with the minimum of time wasted on sleep and food. That was fine for them, no doubt, but my play wasn't of that calibre. I hesitated to partner the Honourable Frederick at all.

"I don't play very well, sir," I reminded him, as he looked about for a table to join.

"Nonsense, Goodale. Just don't take me out of anything if you have at least two little ones, and bid conservatively."

We ended up making a table with a couple of my boss's own class. In fact, the richly bejeweled wife succeeded after a lengthy inquisition in identifying a few people they all knew, at least casually. Her tubby older husband kept reminding her they were there to play cards, not to natter on, but she seemed accustomed to ignoring him.

The Honourable played with every appearance of casualness, replying without hesitation to her sallies. Nonetheless, we won more than our share of the hands, and after three rubbers, our male opponent cried off.

"You're too good for us, I'm afraid."

"Not at all, my good sir," the Honourable assured him. "You can't beat the cards. Maybe your luck will change."

"Not unless my partner does."

"Now, dear!" she reproached him. "It's only a game. You shouldn't take it so seriously."

"I shouldn't have lost track of that last heart, sir," I apologized to my own partner.

"Never mind. As the lady says, it's just a game. Let's go back to the cabin and order tea."

As I wasn't paying for it, I ate heartily, mostly sandwiches and cakes. Then my boss retired for a nap, and I went off to practise my typing, but I made certain to return in plenty of time to get him sorted out in dinner togs. He was insistent that I tie his tie for him, which I'd have wanted to do anyway. Odd that such a bright person, so good at so many things, just could not tie a simple tie.

He took the gloves I handed him but this time not the cane. Would a proper valet try to encourage him to take it? Maybe, but I let it go.

"Now listen, Goodale."

"Yes, sir," I agreed apprehensively.

"You can take some time off, but don't spend it here, and don't come back without telephoning first. It may be a little tough, but here's two quid. Have fun, but stay out. Understood?"

"Very good, sir."

Then he left to find his lady. I got as dressed up as I could. I'd heard chaps complain that their servants pinched their clothes. Well, now I could understand the temptation. Luckily, the Honourable Frederick was taller and narrower in the chest than I was, so it wouldn't have worked.

Probably the secret was to take service with someone your own size.

I gave Winterhaiter a note for Molly and a bob. He was gone nearly half an hour.

"Sorry, sir. She was hard to find. They are all working a bit late down there. She says, if you will wait, she will meet you at the Grill Room as soon as she can get free and change."

"Thank you, Winterhaiter. I shall wait as instructed."

I strolled over to the area outside the Grill Room. I was certainly not going to wait inside and sit there drinking up my capital. The amount was definitely finite.

As I alternately stood and paced, waiting for the appearance of my lady, I noticed one of the crew behaving in a peculiar fashion. He was sort of creeping up the hall. At first I could see no reason for it. Then I saw his objective. It was the cat I had named Rowney.

Abruptly the man started to run forward to grab him. I did my best, and I must say it worked very well. My right foot caught his right foot, and he took a terrific toss, fortunately landing on a thinnish rug.

I hustled forward to help the poor chap.

"Oh, do forgive me! I am most dreadfully sorry!"

The cat was gone, as if he had never been there.

"I do hope you're not hurt!"

"Nope," he replied, looking confused.

"It was entirely my fault," I assured him, as I reached down to help him up. "Please. I really feel terrible about this."

I drew two bob from my pocket and pressed it into his hand. I hadn't meant to give him so much, but if I stopped to count it, it would ruin the act.

At the sight of the silver he seemed to forget everything else. He still looked dazed, but he went away. I'd accomplished my objective. The little voice said, "I always win."

Shortly afterward, Molly appeared sans the high heels but looking very fresh and healthy in the seductively tailored blue dress she'd been wearing when we met. I held out my hand to her. She took it and linked her arm in mine. I was about to escort her into the Grill Room when I was hit by a vertical breeze, so to speak.

Striding down the way was someone I knew, and more to the point, who knew me: Ernest Red. I'd gone to school with this ass. Over six feet tall and orange-haired, he had watery blue eyes and a very active adam's apple. In a dark suit with a white tie covered in tadpole-like black squiggles, he looked like some sort of German punctuation mark. I turned away, but not in time.

"Roddy!" he yelled.

I tried to think of the right word for him. The mental exercise distracted me from panic. "Bumpkin" seemed to fit, but bumpkins are usually nicer. "Ass" was still the mot juste.

"What ho, Ernie," I replied less enthusiastically.

"Oh, ho! Who's this?" he demanded, staring at my lady.

What could I do?

"Oh, Molly, this is someone I went to school with: Ernest Red."

Molly stifled a laugh by turning it into a cough and murmured something polite.

"Well, well, what are you doing now, Roddy?"

Without thinking, I replied, "I am a writer."

"I didn't know he knew how to write!" he told Molly with a guffaw.

"We have to get to our table," I informed him. "We're a bit late. See you about."

I piloted Molly to safety as quickly as possible.

"You aren't serious," she said, when we'd been seated. "His name can't be Ernest Red."

"Yes, it is," I assured her. "I don't suppose his parents ever heard of Communism."

"You don't like him," Molly observed.

"No, I don't. The first day of school he tried to grab a bag of peppermints off me and found out that I did not hold much with his brand of Communism. I got a trifle rough, but it was the last trouble of that sort I had with him."

"Boys will be boys, they say," she remarked.

"He has a big mouth, too," I told her.

Then I realized that I might be giving

something away, just by saying that. Fortunately, Molly had lost interest in Ernie.

"Well, let's leave him be and enjoy ourselves. I think I would like a gin and tonic, if the finances will run to that."

"Oh, yes," I replied, "the very thing."

I loved the way she was careful of my money. It made me feel very warm towards her. Indeed, I had to face up to the fact that I was really getting stuck on this girl. I wondered how the Honourable Frederick was getting on with his Betsy.

I sat back and gazed at the glittering scene: the tables set with linen and crystal, the gaily-dressed couples, the band with their instruments. I wanted to keep this sight as a memory for the rest of my life. Even if I were to bow to my father's wishes, my sea-going experiences in future would not be like this. Molly's frown broke into my glowing dream.

"One of my workmates saw you playing cards with some rich people and the English lord."

Her tone fell between accusation and puzzlement.

"We were playing bridge," I explained, "and not for money."

"Well, how come some servant is playing cards with the high people?"

"Good question," I replied, realizing that it was.

"Well? Have you been promoted to companion or something?"

She was sort of right.

"Do you play bridge?" I countered.

"Who? Me? I'm not rich!"

"You don't have to be rich. You just need a good memory—and three other players. The Honourable Frederick is here on his own, and most of the other passengers seem to be couples. It's much easier for him to get a game, if he doesn't have to wait around for three people to need a fourth. We played tennis as well, something else that's easier with a partner."

"Don't you just leap out calling, 'Anyone for tennis?'"

"I guess you could," I admitted. "You know, Molly, it sort of started when we got onto the boat. Oh, he does let me help him dress and tidy up, but it's not how I'd expect it to be. I know other men who've done this job, and this is not quite it. He talks to me a little, too, about things

I wouldn't expect. He even asks for my opinion. Not what I'd been led to expect. Yes, you're sort of right: I have got promoted, but I don't know why."

"Maybe he just likes you."

"Somehow, that doesn't seem to be enough."

"Well, you talk right. You said that's important to him."

I shook my head.

"Important enough to keep me my job, that's all. No, that's not enough. There's something else. I know he likes this American lady on board. In fact, he seems quite smitten with her."

Molly laughed a little.

"I like that. 'Smitten.' Very old fashioned."

"Well, besotted then."

"Same thing again."

"Nuts about her?" I suggested.

"That is more up to date."

"Anyway, you're right. My position has changed, unofficially, at least."

We ate, the roast beef dinner this time, for the most part in silence, just taking in the atmosphere. Among the dancing couples I noticed the Honourable Frederick with Miss Weston.

In a silky dark-red gown and her hair pinned up, she shone like a beam of moonlight. He held her tightly against him, and they moved to "Love Me or Leave Me" with an easy grace I could only envy. In the end it was Molly who broke the spell.

"I hate to say it again, but I do have to get up early."

"Well, let's have a coffee," I urged.

"No, thank you. It would keep me awake for hours."

"All right. We'll go as soon as I settle up. What's the smallest tip I can get away with?"

"Don't ask me," she smiled. "I'm the lady here."

"Well, off we go. I shall just chance it."

As we left the Grill Room, I noticed that same rat-faced man I had seen before. No! Hey! Wait a minute! It wasn't that I had seen him before. I had imagined him when I was thinking of plots for thrillers. He wasn't real. Was he? Had I lost my mind? Well, someone else could see him this time. A ship's officer was asking him to vacate first class, if he wasn't going to the Grill Room. I thought he gave me and Molly a glance as he departed.

"Who's he?" I asked her, shaken.

"I don't know. We collect hundreds of new people every voyage. I don't try to remember all the ones in third class, and I don't even see most of the others."

Regaining my grip on reality, I decided that I must have seen him before and stored him in my mind as a possible villain without conscious knowledge of it. Maybe writers did that all the time. Did I want to have characters suddenly showing up out of my subconscious and taking over my novels? Wouldn't that be pretty unnerving? Food for thought there, for certain, but I'd be happier not thinking about it.

After I'd escorted Molly to her lift, I went to the Writing Room sort of automatically. It occurred to me that I seemed to be about the only passenger doing much writing, but it was rather late in the evening to be sending postcards home. Probably a rainy afternoon would see it busier.

I sat and wrote in my notebook all that had happened that day and what we had said. I didn't deceive myself that it was of any value in itself, but I needed to become accustomed to a routine of writing—Ann Merrit had said so in her book on being a writer—and I needed to record life on paper so that I could see how it sounded. Did I manage to capture the idea, the essence of what things were like, or did I just jot down facts and talk? I had come to realize in a personal way what on some level the rest of the world already knew: writing is not just recording lists of facts and the words of conversations but communicating the feeling of them to the reader.

If that's more obvious than profound, well, I was just starting to learn the trade, and that always really starts with doing the job, that is, in this case, getting down the material so as to convey it to the reader, if there ever is one.

Perhaps Molly could read it. Well, no, she wouldn't be the best person to try it out on. Hmm.

To collect my thoughts, I looked up from my notebook and across the room. My eyes met Rowney's round, green gaze. He was just sitting there, watching me.

"What ho, Rowney, old chap!" I greeted him. "What do you think about the trip, eh? Glad you came? Wish you'd stayed home? Getting enough to eat, are you? Plenty of mice for all of you?"

He walked over to me. I held out my hand. He sniffed it, arched his back like a shoulder shrug, and walked out.

I then did something of which many might have disapproved. I walked back to the Grill Room and found the waiter who had served our table. He was a Latin type, very smooth and good looking, but his most striking feature was an unusually large bow tie, beautifully tied, definitely not standard issue. I slipped him six-pence to sneak in and pour me a coffee cup full of cream and bring it out to me with an empty saucer. He was a little worried about the crockery, but I promised faithfully to return it. Although the china must have inevitably suffered some breakage from time to time, it was clearly expen-sive and not supposed to leave the Grill Room.

Carefully I walked back to the Writing Room. Not only was the cup full, but the ship had started rolling a bit. I supposed an old sailor like my dad could probably tell just from the way the ship felt exactly what the sea was doing from minute to minute. An odd life.

Back in the Writing Room, I sat down. I didn't see Rowney, so I pushed on with the night's notes. I even steeled myself to type out some of it on the ship's stationery, although I still made a lot of mistakes and didn't get on very fast. I reminded myself to make sure my account was complete, that I wasn't leaving out any details.

That brought to mind detective stories I'd read, and before I knew it, I was thinking of how to get rid of Ernie Red's body. Of course, you could simply push it overboard. If no one saw you, there was a good chance it would pass as an accident. That wasn't very ingenious, though. What about putting the body into a lifeboat and lowering it into the sea? No, that wasn't on. I'd have to go down and unhook the lines holding the boat. Maybe I should sneak down to the engine room and find out when the coal heavers got their tea break, but would the body be sufficiently destroyed before they finished? You wouldn't want some bright lad remarking, "What's this corpse doing in the furnace?"

Killing Ernie in the first place was easier. I rolled a sheet of the ship's stationery into the typewriter and started to list murder methods. Strangling headed the list. I got some satisfaction from typing out a description of how his neck felt in the murderer's hands. I could beat him to death: appealing but too messy. I gave it a sentence anyway. Hitting him on the head was likely to be as messy and less satisfying. Stabbing would be neat, if I left the knife in, but couldn't the police trace the knife? Shooting was out of the question. I'd need a gun with a silencer—unless I could coordinate the shot with a loud ship noise. On the plus side, I could toss the pistol overboard. I was considering poison—if it looked like natural causes, I wouldn't have to dispose of the body—when I became aware of someone entering the room. Whoops! Good thing they couldn't read what I'd been typing; it might seem odd.

Then I saw who the intruder was: Ernie Red! Blimey! I'd been using his name as the murderee. That would seem way past odd. Suavely, I smiled up at him and rolled the paper out of the machine.

"Is that the stunning masterpiece?" he greeted me jovially. "Let's see."

He held out his hand.

"Just some notes. It wouldn't interest you."

I folded the sheet in two with the typing on the inside.

"Oh, come on! I bet it's a love poem to Miss Beautiful, and that's why you don't want me to see it."

"Yes, that's right," I agreed. "Now leave it be. I'm off."

He made a lot of mocking noises. He could not tell he'd gone too far—he never could—but he backed off. I went to the door and glared until he'd definitely retreated.

That was close. I'd have to be more careful in future. Ernie knew me well enough to feel less offended than frightened, if he'd read what I'd typed, and I didn't need someone complaining to the purser that I was planning to murder him.

I went back to considering body disposal methods as I walked down the hall. After a few minutes I circled back and returned to my typewriter. I was still musing on that when Rowney reappeared. Slowly, I got to my feet. I poured half the cream into the saucer and set it on the floor. Then I gave it a little cautious push in his direction. Rowney did a half circle around it and then advanced on his target. He sniffed and decided it was safe. Then he lowered his head and lapped up all of it.

He looked up at me. I picked up the cup and moved toward the saucer. Rowney backed off a bit and waited. I poured the rest of the cream. When I'd retired to my chair, he advanced again and drank all that, too. Then he sat down and washed his hands and face. After about half an hour he tired of my company and strolled off to see what other forms of amusement were going tonight.

By then it was after ten o'clock. I decided I had better check in with my boss, so I handed back the china, thanked my waiter, and rang up the cabin. The Honourable picked up at once.

"Come home, Aunt Cicely."

"Very good, sir," I replied to his weird code.

I wondered what anyone else would think who happened to call. I guess he didn't think anyone else would.

CHAPTER
— 9 —

IT DIDN'T TAKE ME LONG TO REACH THE STATE-room. I opened the door and stopped dead. Our clothes and other belongings were in a bit of a mess, in fact, a hell of a mess.

"What's this?" I exclaimed.

The Honourable Frederick was sitting casually in his favourite chair. He may have tossed things from it onto the floor; it was impossible to tell. As usual, he had a pipe in his hand.

"Oh," he replied, "we had a visitor. He didn't get anything. I put what I had in the purser's safe at the beginning of our voyage."

"How did he get in, sir? The door looks all right."

"Oh, yes, but if you examine the lock closely, you can see scratches where he used a piece of wire to pick it. These locks wouldn't be too difficult to do."

"You know about that sort of thing—sir?"

He smiled thinly.

"Well, not a lot, but I have read a large number of detective stories."

"I've read a lot, too, sir," I admitted, "but I don't always remember the details very well. At any rate, I'd best get this cleaned up."

Not waiting for permission from the boss, I got down to it. I brushed the clothes that had been on the floor and refolded everything and put it away. In less than an hour I had every item in the three rooms back in its place except for one.

"Have yourself a drink, Goodale," the Honourable Frederick instructed.

I did pour out a small brandy and soda.

"Thank you, sir. You were wrong about nothing having been taken."

"What's not here?"

"The briefcase you were kind enough to give me, sir. After I put some typing paper into it,

I closed the catch and could not get it open. I kept forgetting to ask you if you had a key."

"I may have a key with my other ones, but it's too late now. It's of no consequence. It's just an old case. We can easily replace the paper."

I took a deep breath.

"Somehow, sir, that does not make me easy in my mind, if you will pardon my taking the liberty of saying so."

He raised his eyebrows at me.

"You mean someone has robbed you, and you wish to do something about it? I was intending to report the break-in to the purser in the morning."

"Well, sir," I began to object and then caught myself. "Oh, hell, I'm being rather silly. I withdraw my remark."

"No, no, I do see your point, and I understand your urge to play cops and robbers."

"Yes, sir. That's all it amounts to. Let's leave it alone."

"No. Now I am interested. Yes, we could have a little fun at this, and it may take my mind off the lady. Do you know, Goodale, she says she doesn't understand me!"

"Indeed, sir. No doubt your backgrounds are very different."

"But what is there to understand? All that matters is that I love her."

It crossed my mind that it was a bit much to expect your valet to advise you on matters of the heart, but I couldn't bring myself to tell him that, no matter how tactfully worded.

"Perhaps, sir," I ventured, "she finds it hard to accept that you should have developed such a strong attachment on so short an acquaintance."

"A beautiful girl like that? You'd expect all the men she meets to fall in love with her at first sight."

"Well, she may not understand that."

"Why not? I'm not offering to cover her with diamonds, damn it, but I can give her a comfortable life."

"She may enjoy the life she has, sir," I suggested.

"Hard work without security," he pronounced. "Surely she has the sense to see that."

"Some people do feel drawn to the stage, sir."

"The stage! She's a chorus girl, Goodale, not a renowned tragedienne! I offered to buy her a cozy country estate, and she said she was afraid she'd be bored. Bored!"

"What about a townhouse instead, sir? Always lots to do in London."

"You can't raise a family in a townhouse!"

"Ah. You wish a family, sir?"

"Of course I wish a family. Doesn't everyone?"

"Perhaps she thinks, sir, that she's too young to settle down. I've heard that very lovely women often keep putting off those things until it's too late."

"I wish you'd tell her that."

"I could not take such a liberty, sir."

"And she wouldn't listen, damn it all."

"Why don't I get some cocoa, sir? Things often look better in the morning."

"Cocoa? Morning? Don't talk rot, Goodale! You've started the ball rolling and got me interested in this break-in. Come, Watson; the game is afoot!"

"That I do recollect, sir," I told him, happy to be leaving the morass of romance. "Very well, then, we shall not let it drop, and we shall not go to bed."

"The first thing to do is to get a list of all the

first-class passengers. We can cross most of them off, but if any look a bit odd, I may be able to acquire more information."

I must have stared at him dumbly, as he followed this up with a, "Right. Off you go."

I wanted to ask questions, but he'd sort of galloped over me, so I left. At first I was at a loss. Lists of first-class passengers and their cabin numbers were posted in a couple of places, I'd noticed—in glass-fronted, locked boxes, I supposed to prevent the high-spirited or inebriated from defacing them. I was considering how likely it would be for me to be able to remove one of those lists undetected, when I realized that Winterhaiter would be the lad to help me. Trying to give the appearance of aimless wandering, I tracked him down and drew him aside. Then I took out two more of my dwindling silver shillings.

"I need your assistance for something rather unusual," I told him.

He widened his already prominent eyes and raised his eyebrows in wary surprise.

"Oh, don't misunderstand," I added hastily. "I just need a list of the first-class passengers. My boss wants to see who he might know on board, and he doesn't want to stand there reading the posted lists. Besides, he likes to doodle on things."

"Oh!" Winterhaiter's face cleared. "That's all right then. There are always copies lying around in the ship's offices. One won't be missed."

Clearly, he was happy to be able to accept the two bob with no idea that I might be planning something evil that could implicate him. He disappeared briskly and returned in short order with what I'd asked for. As he handed it over, he said, "I know you can't make your boss keep it out of sight, but if anyone does ask where you got it from, it wasn't me. Clear?"

"Very and totally clear," I assured him. "Thank you for your help."

CHAPTER
— 10 —

I RUSHED THE SECRET DOCUMENTS BACK TO headquarters. Well, it seemed like that. Just as I was opening the stateroom door, a ship's officer came by. I casually turned the papers with the printed side against my leg and gave him a smile. He nodded absently and handed me a little printed form. I glanced at it: a notice about life boat drill, with "Life Boat No.18" written on it.

I took it with the papers I'd acquired by incredible cunning and stealth into Mr. Holmes.

Very much awake and full of zeal, he pounced upon them, pencil in hand, and started to go over the list of people. I expected none of them to mean anything to me, except Ernie Red, and was surprised at the Honourable Frederick's apparent greater knowledgeability.

"The vast majority we can just eliminate," he informed me without glancing up. "Look: this is going to take some time. Ah, this list wasn't posted: no drawing pin holes." At that he did raise his eyes. "How much did it cost, and who did you pay off?"

"It cost two shillings, sir, but I can't reveal who took the money."

He gave me a big smile.

"Good man. Stick by your sources. Now, while I'm working on this, the second part is for you to go and find out where this Boat No.18 is. Not only do we need to show up for the drill looking like old hands, but what if the ship sinks before the drill? Right. Off you go," he urged, pointing at the door.

Very well. I already knew he was eccentric. No wonder Miss Weston didn't understand him. Who would? At least this errand was easy. Having consulted one of the posted plans of the ship, I found my way without difficulty to the Boat Deck. I expected to have to hunt around at some length for the correct life boat, but there turned out to be lit-up signs. When you considered it, that made sense. What guarantee did we have that the ship wouldn't sink at night? Wouldn't we be more likely to hit something in the dark?

I walked over to No.18. They all appeared to be covered with canvas. I guess it wouldn't do to have them fill up with rain or spray. My dad had taught me about knots. There was probably one that loosed easily to remove the canvas, or you could cut the cord with a pocket knife. So. That was that.

I stood there for some time just looking out to sea. I'd have expected everything to be pitch black, but the sky and the waves glimmered with constantly changing light. I was trying to sort out something at the back of my mind that kept squirming away from me. The night was pleasant, but after a while, a chilly little breeze sprang up. As I had not brought my coat out with me, I went back in and up to the stateroom.

The Honourable Frederick was still sitting in his chair, pipe in hand. I reported the location of our assigned life boat and the most expeditious way to get there.

"There is a lift, sir, but in a genuine emergency. . ."

"Yes, yes. Stairs are safer and more depend-able. Thank you, Goodale. Well, I have been over the names in first class. There are only two or three that may offer any hope. I shall look into that now. You go to bed and get some sleep."

"Thank you, sir. May I do anything more before I retire? Would you care for some cocoa?"

"No, no, never mind. Just lay out my sleep-wear. Tomorrow I shall decide what to put on tomorrow. Sufficient onto the day, you know. Good night, Goodale."

Obediently, I took out his pyjamas, robe, and slippers. Then I jumped into my own drab pyjamas and under the covers. I thought for a few minutes about how I could be of more service to Rowney and how I could avoid Mr. Red, but I quickly passed out.

CHAPTER
— 11 —

I'D HEARD THAT SOME PEOPLE HAD BIZARRE AND vivid dreams at sea. I appeared not to be among them. I slept very well. When I awoke, I discovered that my boss had ordered omelettes for our breakfast. It was really my job, but he wasn't strong on obeying the proprieties. I reflected that he probably had relatives who would not approve of his pursuing a lady from the stage.

According to the informed schedule, at eleven in the morning the ship's horn sounded one long blast. It crossed my mind that any late sleepers who hadn't got around to reading their notices would be pretty startled. Like good sailors, the Honourable Frederick and I marched out to stand by our life boat. It was one of twenty. In daylight I was surprised to see the size of the things. In movies they were just large rowboats. These could easily each hold fifty people, maybe more. They must have been thirty feet long and rather wide.

"Oh, my gosh!" an elderly American woman standing nearby exclaimed. "You could cross the Atlantic in one of those! It's even got an engine!"

"Yes, madam," replied a ship's officer proudly. "Eighteen horsepower. We're prepared. Not," he added hastily, "that we're likely to need them."

Although I hadn't been seriously worried before, I did feel reassured now. It would take heavy seas to swamp those. On the other hand, I'd never be able to slip a body into one and set it adrift, would I?

With a crowd of the well-to-do and a few hangers on like me, including a bald man with big glasses I'd noticed before, we stood about until a ship's officer came over to us with a clip-board and asked our names. The Honourable Frederick replied for both of us, whereupon the officer checked us off his list. As they said in cadets, "All present and correct."

After the drill we returned to our now Baker Street lair, which gave no sign of having been rifled again. I believe Sherlock was growing a trifle edgy. He passed some time instructing me in the bidding in bridge games, instruction I could certainly profit from, but neither of us had all our attention on bridge. I believed, although he didn't tell me so, that he was waiting for answers to wireless messages he had sent, and indeed, at about one that afternoon, the replies came. He looked at the message without joy.

"No luck, sir?" I ventured.

"No. Oh, well, that is just our first step. I thought it might make things easier, if I could limit the field." He sighed. "Well, enough of our game for a bit."

He went over and pushed the bell for Winterhaiter. When our steward appeared, he sent him off to reserve seats in the Grill Room, and he sent me off with a note to Miss Weston. I could think of easier ways for him to make his arrangements, but he was the boss. I went down to Miss Weston's cabin in second class. This time when I knocked, she was the one who appeared, casually attired in a beige blouse with pink flowers that fit disturbingly well and a silky beige skirt that was almost ankle length and hung in loose folds.

"Oh, the dutiful messenger," she greeted me.

"Yes, Miss," I replied, smiling, and handed her the note.

She read it, looked at me, and winked.

"Sure. I can use some male company. Living with three other women in a small room is rather trying."

"I would have thought, Miss," I ventured, "that the theatre world would have crowded dressing rooms."

"Oh, sure, especially when you start out. If you're lucky, later on you get a separate room the size of a broom closet. Even at the start, though, you aren't stuck with other women all day, no matter how nice they are. Tell me, Goodale, did you ever have to read any Longfellow in school?"

"No, Miss, not that I recall."

"No, probably not. He's an American poet and a little old fashioned now. We had to read The Courtship of Miles Standish. I thought it was pretty far-fetched at the time. Oh, well. At any rate, you can tell Freddie that I would be pleased to lunch with him in the Grill Room, thanks."

She patted my arm as if to say, "Good boy, Rover," and I returned to inform the boss that he was on for a late lunch companion. I helped get him ready, especially tying his tie.

"Thank you," he told me. "Why don't you order yourself some lunch and then try some of the deck games? Remember to call."

Well, I was certainly hungry. I ate as hearty a meal as they offered, ham and cheese sandwiches with chips, and then vacated the stateroom, as instructed. I could not expect Molly to be off duty for hours. I went to the Writing Room to try typing again but remembered I had unfinished business. I couldn't let the side down.

I proceeded to the Grill Room to find my waiter. I didn't see my boss and his date, but I was trying not to be noticed. For cream and some cold beef I gave my waiter a bob and a promise to bring back the dishes undamaged.

Back in the Writing Room I couldn't see Rowney. I didn't worry much, though. If he were like most cats, he'd appear where the food was in his own time. I settled down to work more earnestly. It was an ill-chosen word, but I can't believe that thinking it was responsible for Mr. Red coming in the door.

"Oh, writing the Old Captain?" he asked.

"No," I replied, "just some work I'm doing."

"I didn't know you had to work."

"It's good for the soul, I've been told."

"Oh, I never thought of that. If you have one, I suppose you should feed it," he said, indicating the cat snack, and with this incredible witticism, left.

I gave thanks to the Higher Power that had removed him before I did. A short time later Rowney strolled in and looked up at me as if to say, "Well, what's up, chum?"

I put the beef and cream down for him. This time he did not wait but moved in for the kill at once. He shook the piece of beef in his teeth, as if it had been a mouse. When he'd finished his lunch, he brushed up against my leg. He purred and sort of milled about for a while and then departed on essential cat business.

As I sat back, I realized that Rowney had the right idea: get out and about. With the boss off for lunch and, with luck, etc., I had nothing to do, but the cat had shown me the way. I returned the china. Then, taking a chance, I made a quick move back to the cabin without ringing up first. I grabbed my oldest coat, disordered my hair, which I was still parting on the left side, as instructed, and slipped on some shabby gloves. In the mirror I did look a bit different.

Before the Honourable Frederick could catch me disobeying his orders, I vacated the state-room and strolled down to the second-class part of the ship. I had no idea what I was doing, but this seemed like a good start. Some frightfully bright chap once said, "If you don't know where you're going, it don't matter what road you take to get there." At least I think that's what he said.

The idea was sound, anyway. After I'd wandered aimlessly about for a while, I combed my hair straight back and took off the jacket and gloves. I admit that wasn't as good as a false nose or a glue-on beard, but if you're casual about such minor changes, people who aren't watching for you specifically will just not notice you.

I saw him on my third trip about the second-class decks: the rat-faced man I had seen being asked to leave the first-class deck. That was just about the time the briefcase must have been stolen. I wanted to do something about this without waiting for the Honourable Frederick to take charge. I wanted to do it myself. It was personal.

Looking back, I can see that I didn't do the wise or sensible thing. I acted like a chap in a book. First off, I had to admit to myself that I could not do this entirely alone. I went back up to first class and tracked down Winterhaiter. He was too busy to be interested in a long explanation. I described whose cabin I wanted to locate in second class, and he ran down and asked a couple of second-class stewards. I was lucky the man was so distinctive looking. It took him very little time to bring back the dope on him. He was Mirabow, Jon Mirabow, and he gave me his cabin number.

While Winterhaiter had been gone, I had devised a plan of action. Admiral Nelson would have shaken my hand and patted me on the back. Well, he still had one hand.

"Do you know when the second class has its life boat drill?" I asked.

"Yes, sir. They had it yesterday."

"Thank you," I told him and handed over two

more of my dwindling supply of coinage.

The boss had said he would cover the last payout, but he hadn't yet. I had no doubt that he would. If needed, I would ask him politely. As to the current payout, I was afraid I was on my own.

I went to the Writing Room, reflecting that I seemed to be spending more time there than in my cabin. On this occasion there was an older woman, apparently writing a letter, but she ignored me. I took a sheet of the ship's stationery and rolled it into a cone shape. In one of the drawers I found a roll of tape and put a piece of it on the cone to make it keep the shape. With a pair of scissors from the same drawer I cut off the pointed end. So far, so good.

I'd intended to seek out my pet waiter at the Grill Room, but I must have struck a break between lunch and tea because there was no one around. Just beyond the gold-coloured rope barrier a table held a group of silver salt and pepper shakers, probably waiting to be redistributed after filling. It was the work of a moment to reach in and swipe two pepper shakers. I slipped them into my jacket pocket, put my jacket back on, and strolled away.

I returned to second class and looked around. Rat-face wasn't where I'd seen him before. As it wasn't meal time, he was likely in his cabin. I went there. Nearby, I found a corner where I could turn my back as if sorting through my pockets for a cigarette or match. Instead, I held the small end of my paper cone and carefully emptied into it the two pots of pepper.

Right. Now it got iffy. Success hinged on that life boat drill the day before. Steadily holding my pepper gun, I walked over to his door and knocked.

"What?" he answered gruffly.

"Sir, your life boat number has been changed. I must give you the notice."

"Put it under the door."

Hmm. I could have claimed orders to place it into his hands, but when I glanced at the way the doors were constructed on the lower decks, I found I could say quite truthfully, "I can't, sir. The doors are different from on land. There is a water barrier at the bottom."

"Oh, all right," he grumbled, and he came and opened the door.

It was working! I was ready for him. When he

opened the door, I put the end of the cone to my lips and blew a great cloud of pepper into his little eyes. He made a strange noise and, hands over his face, stepped back, sneezing violently.

I strode straight past him. I could have struck him on the back of the head to give me time to search, but there, right on the table near the door, was my briefcase. I grabbed it. Without saying anything nasty, triumphant, or flippant, I just sashayed out of the place at the double quick.

I'd been too concerned with the mechanics of the briefcase retrieval to feel more than somewhat nervous beforehand. I hadn't given a lot of consideration to any aftermath, merely reasoning that I should take a roundabout route back to the stateroom in case Mirabow came after me. Now I realized that I hoped he would. To my shock, I felt more exhilarated than ever before in my life. My heart was racing. I was sweating. I'd been in my share of childish punch-ups before, but this was my first unprovoked physical assault, and I felt terrific. The power of the elation frightened me. It told me something about myself I didn't want to face, and I certainly didn't want my cool boss to see it. I couldn't go back until I'd calmed down.

I did pursue a roundabout way back to first class. This was, however, not a brilliant, carefully planned retreat route. Preoccupied, I'd got rather lost and had to meander about for a while. I can't stress enough what a large ship it was.

In truth, Rat-face had little reason to pursue me. I thought that he must have discovered by then that the case contained nothing of value. Still, it might not be prudent to return immediately to our stateroom, if for no other reason than that I might lose my job. Accordingly, I sought refuge in the Writing Room while my heart slowed down. The letter-writing lady had left, so I had it to myself again. I couldn't even see Rowney anywhere.

I sat down at the back of the room, facing the door. As I set the briefcase on the table in front of me, I could tell it wasn't empty. I looked at the lock. I'd assumed it was just one of the easy ones you could open with a hair pin, but I'd been wrong. You really would need a key. I could even see scratches where Rat-face had tried. Now that I came to think about it, I couldn't quite get all this. The boss might enlighten me later. At present I had to own to being fogged.

As I sat in the Writing Room, trying to think out what to do next, a group of four good-looking but not young women drifted in, chattering about the postcards they had to write and what they'd say to whom.

"Don't let us drive you away," one of the women apologized, when I stood up to leave.

"Not at all," I assured her politely. "I'd finished my typing."

I certainly couldn't get much thinking done in company with that lot, but there really was only one thing to do. I went to the nearest ship's phone and asked for the stateroom.

"You may return, Aunt Clementine," the boss said in his usual odd way.

"Very good, sir," I dutifully replied.

I didn't exactly hurry back. Not only did I not wish to be surprised by Rat-face around some corner, but I was puzzling over what to say—and what not to say—about the briefcase and its recovery.

When I entered, the Honourable Frederick

put down the newspaper he'd been reading and glanced at me lackadaisically. He picked up his pipe. Then he caught sight of what I was carrying.

"Holy hell!" he cried. "Where? What? You got it!"

Well, I'd certainly surprised him.

I put the briefcase on the table and said modestly, "Yes, sir, I recovered it."

"How? Who had it?"

"A person named Jon Mirabow, sir, in second class."

"Whatever led you to him?"

"He has a face rather like a rat, sir. I happened to recall that at about the time the case must have been stolen, I saw him being asked to leave the first-class deck. That did not mean anything at the time, but after I found out what had happened—and you had eliminated the first-class passengers—I realized there was a good chance he was the man. Lucky he was so noticeable."

"Probably you were less lucky than observant."

"Possibly so, sir," I granted.

There was a pause.

"Well?" he urged impatiently. "Come on! Out with the tale! I want to hear it."

"Well, sir, I read in a detective story once, I think it was one of Dingwall's, how upsetting pepper can be if used properly, and the author gave a simple method for delivering it to its destination."

"How?"

I took the little cone and passed it to him. I noticed that a few grains of pepper still clung to the paper. He looked at it and frowned.

"Did you just blow it like a bugle?"

"Exactly, sir, and it worked. While he was incapacitated, I dashed in and grabbed the case, which was on a table out in the open not far from the door. I assume he was just getting down to opening it. It looked like he was having trouble with the lock. Why he didn't just cut it open, I don't know. Maybe he hadn't got around to it."

"Maybe," the boss corrected, "he was told not to open it, but his curiosity overcame him, and he couldn't keep himself from trying."

"But what would be in it that was worth a risk of any kind?"

"Nothing, of course. The case had my initials on it, so he assumed it was mine. Unfortunately for him, the items he was after are in the purser's safe. You'd think he'd realize that I wouldn't carry such things about when I didn't have to, but I suppose he may have thought that it wouldn't hurt to explore the possibility."

I felt I should reply, "Indeed, sir," without raising an eyebrow and leave matters like that, but I simply couldn't do it.

"May I ask what all this is about, sir?" I blurted. "After all," I added quickly, "I am now in it, too."

"You're quite correct," he agreed, rather grimly, I thought. "It's very simple: I am taking some official papers from the British government to the United States government."

"So you gave me that briefcase as a decoy—sir."

"No, no, I assure you. It just worked out that way, and not a bad thing."

"Indeed, sir? Then how did you know I wasn't in league with the rat-faced man to get the papers?"

"Oh, I checked you out before I hired you. Your trek across London gave me plenty of time, but as it turned out, it was very easy. The man I asked to do it had served under your father a few years ago. Small world, isn't it?"

"He knew my dad?"

"Yes, that's right. Oh," he assured me, "I did check to be sure of his son's name and found out where you'd gone to school and so on."

"Oh, bloody hell!" I exclaimed, disconcerted. "Oh. Pardon my vulgar outburst. I'm just having trouble taking all this in—sir. So you are not pursuing this Miss Weston to New York at all! No wonder she thought you didn't ring true."

The Honourable Frederick sighed.

"No, no, no. It's not that simple. Is anything ever? I had to take this ship. The official handling me booked this grand stateroom before the New York troop ever got the boot. Would I have booked an inside cabin? Believe it or not, I thought it was good luck that I happened to be able to continue seeing her. I thought it gave me another chance."

"Well, doesn't it, sir?"

I wasn't sure I believed him.

"It doesn't seem to be turning out that way. Betsy's suspicious of me. I told you that, and it's quite true. Her infernal women's intuition, I suppose. I don't know what she thinks I am—maybe Jack the Ripper, maybe just an ordinary ax murderer—but she can't seem to trust the genuineness of my suit, and the more time we spend together, the less good it does. If she had much else to do, I doubt if she'd keep seeing me at all."

That certainly chimed with what she'd told me, but I didn't say so.

"I see," I muttered. "Well, it does all start to make some sort of sense. I'll try not to ask any more questions—sir."

"Damn it, man. Without meaning to, I have acted as if you were part of this, and now you certainly are, even if you would prefer not to be."

I'd been examining my feelings as he spoke, and I found the initial negative ones retreating.

"Oh, no, sir," I heard myself reply. "This is great. Count me in."

Maybe one day, I thought, I could write about it.

"Good," he smiled. "It'll be better now we know where we are. We won't make mistakes from misunderstanding."

"I guess my getting the briefcase back could make Rat-face certain of its importance, sir."

"And not a bad thing, really." He took out his note case. "Here. I owe you some money. Miss

Weston noticed you've acquired a girlfriend. It would seem strange if you didn't buy her chocolates and flowers."

I stared at the ten pound note he handed me.

"Thank you, sir, but how is a valet supposed to afford all that?"

He chuckled.

"It may be cynical of me, Goodale, but I haven't found that women care much where money comes from, so long as it does come."

"You don't know Molly, sir," I pointed out. "Oh, well, I should be able to pretend to be still counting the pennies."

"Oh, counting pennies is always a good thing. Molly, eh? A nice name. There's a song about a Handsome Molly. Let's see if I can find the right key, so you can retrieve your paper."

"Wouldn't it be better, sir, if there were something in the briefcase?"

"Good point. Stick in this," he said, handing me the ship's newspaper he'd been reading.

As it happened, he did not have the right key on the ring he carried about with him.

"I haven't used that case for quite a while," he explained. "I haven't even used my new one all that often lately. I think I shoved my old key chain into my trunk."

This was a big thing with lots of small drawers. He'd insisted on keeping it in his bedroom.

Apparently, Mirabow hadn't tried to open it. He must have assumed he'd found what he was looking for. Searching through it might take some time. While I waited, I decided to try to open the briefcase like Mirabow. The Honourable kept a piece of copper wire about to clear out his pipe stems. I borrowed it and tried poking into the lock to see if anything moved. It didn't. This was a real lock, all right. I didn't take long to confess myself defeated.

Luckily, chance came to the rescue. From the next room the Honourable Frederick shouted triumphantly, "What ho!" and emerged at a gallop, key in hand.

Even with it, opening the case took a bit of doing. I suspect Mirabow and I had upset the delicate mechanism with our amateur foolery. In the end, however, click it went, and at last I had my typing paper.

CHAPTER
— 12 —

AFTER ALL THAT FUSS, I DID FEEL THE JOY OF accomplishment for a few seconds, and then a bucket of ice water chucked over it, as I realized that I had just lost a good excuse for not bothering any more with the typing contraptions. I put the ship's newspaper into the case and sat back, a bit done in. I hesitated to close it up. After all, it had been hard to get open. On the other hand, we had no real reason ever to open it again. Right. I clicked it shut.

"Well," my boss remarked, "we're past the halfway-across mark. Let's see if we can get New York on the wireless."

"Is that possible, sir?"

"Oh, yes. It's tied in with the ship's antenna."

After he got the set warmed up, he fiddled about until, with a sudden burst of sound, a spritely band came out loud and clear, playing something I'd never heard before. When it ended, an announcer said in a non-BBC manner, "That was Glen Gray and his Casa Loma Orchestra playing the "Casa Loma Stomp.""

I'd been out of touch with the English-speaking world for a while, and this was new to me.

"Casa Loma's a place?"

"It's a castle in Toronto," he explained casually. "They use it for dances and so on."

"Toronto is in Canada, sir."

"Bravo, but the band is well known. They often play their stuff on New York and other stations."

"Well, live and learn, sir. What do you want to do now?"

"I'm going to send you with a note to Miss Weston to see if she wants to dance tonight. They start at 9:30."

"Very good, sir, and I call before I come home, as before."

"Yes, as before."

While he was writing the note, I put the

typing paper in my room but left the briefcase out in plain view. Then I stood waiting. When he handed me the note, I slipped it into a ship's envelope I'd found in a drawer when I was tidying up. That would make it look a bit nicer. I left the stateroom for second class.

No, I had not forgotten Rowney. I planned to hit the Grill Room on my way back.

I did keep an eye open for Old Mirabow but saw him not.

When I knocked on the fair lady's cabin door, a red head appeared, then popped back in.

"No, it's not him. It's yours, Betsy."

After a brief wait, Miss Weston herself came out in a very frilly sky-blue dress that looked a bit old-fashioned but suited her. She wore a small round hat. She had applied only a deft touch of make-up and looked pretty enough but not too glamourous.

"Oh," she greeted me. "It's the gallant message carrier."

"Yes, that I am," I agreed and handed over today's effort.

She read it and said, "Well, I like dancing, and he is good at it. The answer is yes, I should be pleased to. He knows my abode and may call."

"Very good, Miss. I shall relay this to him at once."

As I turned to go, she touched my arm.

"Hold on a bit, chum."

"Yes, Miss?"

"Look, I'm all dolled up for a walk on the Promenade Deck, and I need a man to walk with. Why don't you volunteer? It would be your good deed for the day."

I was not at all reluctant, but I did hesitate. Then I reflected that I was no competition for the Honourable Frederick. She was very pretty, and I didn't want to let her down with a refusal.

"I would be honoured to escort you, Miss," I told her and held out my arm.

"Wow!" she smiled. "Freddie never talks like that, and he's a lord or something big."

"He's an Honourable, Miss, the brother of an earl."

"Not such a big deal, then. I don't get all this title stuff."

"It can be quite complicated, Miss. Depending on his exact family situation, the Honourable Frederick may become an earl one day. I did know an Honourable once, though, who calculated that he'd have to polish off nine chaps to get the title. He spoke in jest, of course."

"I should hope so," she replied. By then we'd reached the boat deck. She smiled around, nodding at people she seemed to know, maybe from her troop. "I like ships. My dad was in the US Navy, a captain. He's retired now."

"Really?" I exclaimed. "My father was a captain in the Royal Navy. He's retired now, too, and plays at being a sort of Farmer in the Dell."

She laughed. She had a nice laugh.

"Oh, my dad started a business making sailboats, runabouts, and like that. I've never paid that much attention to it—it sounds real technical—but I think he likes it better than the service. He was always grumbling about conditions and pay and problems and people—when he was at home at all. You know what I mean."

"I must own that I do," I admitted.

He can't care much about her being on the stage, I reflected, but that was none of my concern. We cruised along the Promenade Deck with other people out to have a stroll on a sunny afternoon and to be seen doing it. It wasn't too crowded, though. Sort of fun, really, I felt.

After a while, however, I told her, "I really must take a reply back to the Honourable Frederick. It's what he sent me for, and he will be pacing up and down, saying, 'He cometh not.'"

"Oh. Well, I see your point, but how is the lady supposed to feel—dumped, and by a subordinate, no less?"

"True, too very true, but I promise to make it up to you in the fullness of time. Anyway, my art is calling me."

"Don't tell me you paint pictures?"

"No, I write my paintings."

"Under such pressure, I must release you. Thank you, kind sir, for giving me such a large slice of your valuable time."

She removed her hand from my arm and waved me away as if I were a serf. I had no time to stop at the Grill Room but proceeded at the double quick back to the stateroom.

I said as I went in, "She says yes, of course, she would love to come, sir."

My boss looked up from cleaning his pipe.

"It took a while for you to extract that from her," he remarked.

"Yes, sir. She made me walk her along the Promenade Deck so she could show off her new frock."

"I hope you enjoyed it," he replied. "I'm off to that dining room. I suggest you order something, but don't dally here too long."

"Permit me, sir," I said, and stepped forward to adjust his tie.

I smiled at my petty concerns. He nodded and left. It struck me that, if we parted company, I would miss having to tie his tie. Funny, isn't it, what you grow accustomed to? Well, if I moved sharply, I could get some jobs done before dinner. I rolled up some typing paper, stuck it into my jacket pocket , and marched to the Grill Room, where I found my pet waiter, who came up with the needful. He palmed my money with an expert elegance that you'd have to have seen to appreciate—or perhaps "understood" would be a better term, as he could have succeeded as a conjuror.

I returned to the Writing Room. I was going to start my masterpiece, and I had the paper to do it on. I would no longer be daunted, even if there were dozens of old ladies writing cards.

There weren't. In fact, I had the place to myself, not surprising during the dinner hour.

I sat down at my corner machine and rolled in page one. The paper started to go in crooked, so I had to roll it out and try again. That was better. I thought deeply for a moment. Then I uttered a heartfelt prayer and typed "The Liner Murder Mystery "across the top, underlined it boldly, and on the right put "Page One."

At that point Rowney appeared, flicking his ears at me in annoyance that I was so late. I put down the beef on a posh china plate. He made straight for it and started in. It made me feel grand to be privileged to feed such a glorious representative of God's creation. I set down the cream and watched him lap it up.

Oh, well, back to work, eh? I hadn't decided on the time of the year to write about. I thought winter would be dramatic, with stormy seas and so on, but then probably everyone except the most seasoned sailors would be lying in their bunks, seasick and wishing for the end. Not good. On our ship we had so far been lucky: no heavy seas or wild storms. It also occurred to me that I hadn't thought up a name for my hero. For now I decided to call him

Rodney. I could alter it later. I'd heard that authors sometimes have to rewrite. Some of the lads back at my pub in London seemed to rewrite all the time. I wondered if Shakespeare had ever had to. Probably not.

"You're feeding a cat!"

I turned from the typewriter to see Molly standing by the door. She wore purple this time, but still the tailored look that suited her so well. Her sternness also suited her. In fact, everything suited her. She was simply a gorgeous woman. I could have stared at her forever.

"Well, yes," I admitted, when I'd caught my breath. "He was hungry."

"In this world there are millions of people hungry—starving!—and you choose to feed an animal?"

"I didn't happen to see any starving people on my way from the Grill Room."

"Don't you be flippant! There are people in desperate need, and you choose to spend your money on a cat!"

Having cleaned the dishes, Rowney had removed himself into a corner. I couldn't blame him. As far as he was concerned, Molly was redundant.

"Well," I reasoned, "I don't know all those people, but I know that cat, and I like him, so I feel he has a claim on me."

"Right! Feudalism! I see, and what happens when you leave this ship in a couple of days? Have you thought of that?"

"Not in any detail," I confessed, "but I shall do something—on my word of honour," I said to Rowney.

"He can't understand you! He's just an animal!"

"He may get the general idea," I objected. "Cats are very smart."

"Well, he certainly knows a sucker when he sees one."

"I think of him as a pal."

"A pal? A cat? I don't understand your attitudes at all, Rodney! You spend what little money you make on a scruffy feline!"

"Oh, that's not fair! Rowney's not scruffy! He's a handsome cat."

"You have a silly job, and you think you're going to be a writer."

"What's silly about being a valet?"

"Why don't you get a real job? In a factory or

painting houses? Something manly."

"In case you haven't noticed, the capitalistic swine have destroyed the economy very effectively. Manly jobs anyone could do have long queues for them. I was very lucky to get the job I've got—and for that matter, so are you."

Molly thought she was going to say something in reply but changed her mind. She probably couldn't think of anything good enough on the spur of the moment. We all have that problem.

"Well," she said more mildly, "let's not argue. Are you going to take me out tonight?"

"Yes, certainly, if you will be so good as to go. I wasn't sure until the last minute that the boss wouldn't need me."

"I don't know now," she reflected. "One of my mates in second class saw you with his lordship's girl, walking the Promenade Deck, arm in arm."

"Yes," I replied happily. A little jealousy wasn't a bad thing, was it? Maybe she wasn't as put out as she'd sounded. "She's a nice person. The Honourable seems to confuse her not a little."

"Great heavens! She's a show girl! She can't be very bright."

"Well, she seems to be more intelligent and

better educated than one would expect."

"No matter to us, anyway. Shall I meet you outside the Grill Room—at nine, say?"

"Great. I should get these dishes back there soon."

Molly recoiled in horror.

"Don't tell me I could have been eating off a plate that a cat used?"

"Of course not," I lied. "These have been set aside especially for me to use for Rowney."

"Good. That's better. I shall see you later then."

Out she went, looking lovely. I returned to the novel. I still did not have a name for the hero, but his sidekick was to be Rick Blewitt, a short little man who found things out for the hero so that I wouldn't have to dream up ways to do it. Coincidence is not my style in detective fiction. The evil murderer I would call Magellan. It sounded like that kind of a bloke. I couldn't remember where I'd heard that name before, but it seemed to fit.

I started to type the opening lines of the novel. I was happy to notice that I didn't have to look so hard to find the keys I wanted. At the end of the page I rolled it out and picked up Rowney's plates. Well, I had made a start, but I couldn't for the life of me see where it should go at this point. I guess I'd have to think out the story a bit past just the idea of a killer on a boat. A plot: that was what I needed. Yes, I would have to work that out. I handed the plates in to the waiter and gave him sixpence because he smiled at me. Sometimes I'm a bit silly.

I'd intended to write more, and now I had a little time to myself. That was another problem: if there was a killer, who would he kill? I went to the boat deck and wandered about a bit. The first thing I noticed was a group of sailors taking the canvas off a life boat, so that some sort of petty officer could check that the oars, water, etc., were all there and the boxes of emergency rations were replaced. I hadn't known about this. It meant I couldn't have chaps hiding corpses in life boats, at least for very long, and even for short periods of time they'd need to know the inspection schedule or be lucky. There's always a snag. Of course, that could be how the murder was discovered, couldn't it? Hmm.

It seemed about time to go to the Grill Room,

so I went. Molly appeared after I had actually finished and butted a cigarette, so I did not have to waste one. The Honourable Frederick would have been proud of me for thinking like that.

"Good evening, Molly," I greeted her. "You look radiant."

She smiled. I had said the right thing first crack. Good show. Keep it up. Mind you, it was the simple truth. She was still wearing her purple dress, but she'd fancied it up with a flashy gold pendant in the shape of a sunburst. Despite her blue eyes, looking more than ever like the North Sea, Molly had the rich, deep-toned complexion of the brunette. No doubt she did use some lip rouge and powder, but her glow was natural. Betsy, in contrast, as a blonde, tended to look a bit like a white mouse without all of her makeup. Dressed to go out for the evening, though, she was a fairy princess. Rummy creatures, women.

The nice waiter I had tipped lavishly for the sake of a cat found us a table not too close to the band, which had started on the dance music, although so far in a rather subdued way. "Love Me or Leave Me" seemed to be a favourite. Both of us were familiar with the menu. We ignored possible additions and changes and just ordered the roast beef. We'd had it before and knew it was very good. I reflected that I should try to remember what some of the French dishes were called so that I could ask my boss later what they were. I noticed the bald man in the big glasses at the next table, writing something on the menu.

"What are you and his lordship going to do when we hit New York?" Molly asked.

"He hasn't told me his plans. I'll be happy just to get there. I've never been to the States before. I assume we shall pursue the dancing lady, but it may not pan out that way."

"What do you really think of her?"

"Well, she seems nice. She dresses well and doubtless knows all the makeup tricks, what with being on the stage."

Molly looked thoughtful for a bit. Then the food arrived, and she dug in. Although she would have been mortally offended if I'd said so, she ate like Rowney. I suspect the crew's meals were not quite up to this level of excellence.

We sipped the rather good red wine they had supplied with the meal. Well, it was better than they served in The Frozen Inkpot. I started to glow with a feeling of well-being. She torpedoed that with her next remark.

"Have you given any thought at all to settling down to a real job with a future to it? This valet thing is just for the present."

"Well," I admitted, "truth to tell, the Honourable Frederick has sacked a fair number of valets in his time, but when I saw the sort of people they'd been sending him, it did not surprise me that they did not get on with him."

Molly sniffed.

"Probably good, honest, working people."

"Could be, but not the ones to please a slightly different sort of person like him."

"Different?"

"Yes. He's very much his own man. If you want to advise him, it helps to be careful how you put it."

"And he's getting along with this showgirl?"

"I thought so, but the girl is not helping."

"She's just staying aloof to keep him interested," she scoffed.

"Could be, I suppose, but I'd say they are two people who just will not get along. They're too different as individuals, and they come from very different sorts of backgrounds."

I slammed the brakes on my big mouth. I was about to say that she came from a Navy background like me. Would Rodney the detective make such a near blunder? Never; he's too cagey.

Molly dropped her eyes and then raised them to mine.

"Well, Rodney, to be honest with you, I think we share the same problem: we are too different."

My heart sank.

"But that could be a positive thing," I asserted. "We won't bore each other."

She waved that idea aside.

"Oh, don't think I haven't thought this out properly. I have—really. Yes, we can get along, even have some fun, but I need more than that. There isn't any sort of fire. Don't you see?"

"I'm dull," I interpreted.

"Oh, Rodney," she said earnestly, "don't take it too hard. We just don't match. It's like a skirt and a jumper when the colours simply do not go together, even though the quality of each is fine."

"So we end this tonight?"

"Oh, not like that!" she entreated. "We can go

on being friends, can't we? I just wanted you to understand that that's as far as it goes. It wouldn't be fair to give you the wrong idea. Besides," she added with a smile she probably intended to soften her words, "I really love to dance, and you can't dance at all."

That struck me as a pretty stupid reason to ditch a chap. I could learn, after all. The truth was: she just did not want me. Worse, I could see her point.

"Yes," I replied reluctantly, "I suppose you're right all the way down the line. Well, let me pay the bill, and then I'll go see what I must do before we dock."

"It's not that urgent. We should not be too far from New York tomorrow, but we usually have to wait for a ship to clear the docks." Molly was happy to move onto a more neutral topic. "There are only so many that can handle a passenger ship of this size, and then there are customs people and all that." She took a deep breath. "At any rate, before too long you are off the ship and launched into New York society."

"Yes," I agreed, trying to take some pleasure in the prospect.

We parted outside the Grill Room with smiles and the sort of girl's handshake that doesn't mean much. I sneaked back in and found my waiter. I had to stand about for a while to get him, as the staff were all busy, but he got meat and cream for me, and I paid him more than enough.

As I walked back to the Writing Room, a voice said, "I always win."

Well, I didn't feel like a winner. The girl had just given me the bird, however she'd tried to sugar-coat it. I did have an idea, but I wasn't sure how to work it.

In the Writing Room I lit a cigarette and sat thinking for a while. Then I turned over a sheet of ship's stationery to the blank side and drew a plan of what I wanted, carefully noting down the dimensions.

Rowney had been watching. When he knew the way was clear, he walked in and said, "Hi!"

That is, a small meow. He sat and looked at me. I got out his dinner and set it down for him. He seemed less hungry than before, but he ate all of it and licked up every last drop of cream. Then he strolled over and waited for me to pat him. Persians often have extra padding, but I could feel each rib distinctly.

"Poor Rowney," I murmured.

He rubbed against me and then sauntered off with his tail up. That was the answer: keep your tail up.

"Thanks, Rowney!" I called after him.

I had a good laugh at myself. Then I typed an opening scene in which Rodney gets a call from a woman with a seductive voice and a strange foreign accent. I still had my book to write.

I thought I should check to see if the boss was back, so I went to the phone and rang up the stateroom. No luck. I gathered up the papers and plates. The papers I put into my pockets, and I took the plates back to my food assistant, to give him a more important title. There's a lot in titles. Ask the Honourable Frederick.

Leaving the Grill Room, I had the good luck to encounter my second target.

"Mr. Winterhaiter, sir, a moment, please."

"Yes, sir?" he replied with a smile and a hopeful glint in his prominent eyes.

"I assume on a vessel of this size there's a ship's carpenter?"

My dad's ships always had them.

"Yes, sir. There are two."

"Could one of them make me something simple, if I give him a drawing?"

"Don't see why not. Joe'd be the one for that. He's more creative, like."

"Good. Here is the drawing." I handed it to him with a coin. "Take the shilling for your trouble and find out how much he wants to make it. I need it fast, understand?"

"Yes, indeed. We'll be in New York Harbour before too long. Docking can take a while, though."

"So I was told."

He had just stepped on my sore ego. Well, never mind. I let him go on his errand while I went to a telephone and rang up our GHQ again.

"Come home, Aunt Lavinia," said the voice.

I understood the code.

"Yes, sir, at once," I replied.

A bit too much walking to the stateroom for "at once," really, but I made it as soon as I could, as he sounded rather down. When I arrived, I found my employer in his chair fooling with his pipe.

"Goodale," he greeted me with a frown. "Glad

to see you. Have a chair. We have a change of plans thrust upon us by higher powers."

"Yes, sir?" I replied blankly.

"Indeed, yes. I just received a radiogram from my boss. We are not to land at all. We wait on board. The British Ambassador's office will be sending someone to collect the documents I'm in charge of. We will make a safe transfer in the purser's office. After that we shall not be needed, or, indeed, wanted. So. We do not get to land and see New York City, I regret to say."

I was stunned. I felt like a runner who trips a few yards from the finish line. I didn't know what to say.

"That is, of course, not all," he continued. "The next bad luck is that Miss Weston has given me the bird—again. If I could follow her into town, maybe I could talk her around. I've done it before, but she and the rest of the company will be leaving the ship as soon as we tie up, and I won't."

He paused. I felt I had to say something.

"This was not at all expected, sir. I admit to being at a loss."

"One way out for you would be to quit me now and go on into New York yourself. Have a look at the place for a week or so. You must have some money to get home, of course."

"No, sir," I heard myself say. "Even if I did have some money, I would not leave you in these circumstances." He put down his pipe and looked at me. "Maybe fate will find a way to help us along," I suggested. "At any rate, I suppose we must look our best when the officials come. Let me get out the boot polish now and set to work. You know, I've found working with one's hands can relieve one's mind and sort out one's thought processes, too."

"For whatever good that may do," he sighed. "Well, you do that, and I'll try a quick spin on the Promenade Deck. The fresh air won't hurt, and maybe I shall meet some sweet young girl out there. Who knows?"

"Well, sir," I confessed, "the lady I was running after gave me the bird tonight, too."

He stared.

"Surely you jest! We can't both have been scuppered on the same boat on the same evening! These things don't happen in real life!"

Well, I'd startled him out of some of his depression. That was something, I guess.

"It has happened, sir. Maybe in the enclosed

society of a ship it has more of a chance to happen than in a city or town."

"Yes, Goodale, you could have a point," he granted. "You do seem to think things through. I knew you were a bright lad when I first saw you. At any rate, let us to our duties go, eh, what?"

"Indeed, sir."

He knocked out his pipe in the ashtray and cleaned it with a little metal tool. While he went for his spin, I got out the shoe-polishing para-phernalia, and soon I had his footwear and the entire cabin shipshape and Bristol fashion. It did seem to help a bit, as did the Honourable's walk.

He returned looking rather refreshed and sat down again with his pipe.

"Don't you think you'd be better off in bed?" he suggested.

Or, to put it more straightforwardly: out of the way. As I was a bit tired, I more than agreed with the agenda.

CHAPTER
— 13 —

My first thought on awaking was how very quiet it was. When I got dressed, I noticed that the Honourable Frederick was still asleep. With no instructions to wake him, I went out to get him a ship's paper. The ship was definitely moving very slowly. I wondered if that was because of coming into port, and then I heard the fog horn. They do sound mournful. Curious, I stepped out onto the deck and into a grey blanket almost as wet as a swimming pool. This was no mere mist but a real London fog of the best or the worst type. I couldn't see very far at all, only a few inches. I'd glimpse a stanchion or a stretch of railing, and then the swirling cloud would cover it again. I had no reason to doubt the skill of our driver, but I couldn't help feeling a bit apprehensive.

I ducked back in, bringing a drift of wet air with me. It did not appear that I'd be seeing much of New York, even from the ship. Well, I had more important concerns. I tracked down Winterhaiter, who asked me for one pound for the carpenter's work and one shilling for the wood and other material. I gave him the money, and he promised to make delivery very soon. I paid him another sixpence, and he bustled off.

Preoccupied, I wandered back to the stateroom and found the occupant beginning to stir. When I brought in his tea, he took it but told me to order a pot of coffee with breakfast.

"Yes, sir. I'm afraid we're in a real peasouper of a fog, sir," I reported.

"Oh, that's why we're moving like a funeral procession," he deduced. "Oh, well. Have my best things dug out anyway. It may be later than expected, but I shall still have to meet those chaps sometime today."

"Yes, sir. I was hoping we could at least see the Statue of Liberty, but that's likely to be completely out of the running."

"Well, it is big, but I'm not much for statues."

In his shiny grey silk dressing gown he wandered into the living room and started assembling his pipe of choice and poking about for his tobacco pouch.

Breakfast arrived more quickly than I'd expected, but it couldn't be too soon for me. I'd gone a little light on the food the day before, so I jumped in. The Honourable Frederick didn't show much interest in anything except coffee. He ate half a slice of toast with a little marmalade and pushed away the tray. To demonstrate my enthusiasm for economy, I finished off the rest, including two bowls of porridge.

"Si jeunesse savait," he muttered with a half-smile and settled down with his pipe and paper. After I laid out his clothes, I couldn't help hovering a bit, I admit. I thought there must be more I should be doing, but I could hardly pack when we weren't leaving, could I?

"Will there be anything further, sir?" I asked.

He waved me away.

"No, no. Take a walk. Enjoy the fog."

I thought that was a great idea. I scurried down to the boat deck for another look at the life boats. I wanted to work them into my mystery, but I couldn't see exactly how to do it. Then I went to the second class Promenade Deck, sort of half hopefully, I guess.

As I stood there, I heard women's laughter approaching. It was rather strange. I could even smell their perfumes before I could see them, a whole bunch of women, invisible. Of course, they couldn't see me, either. I had to step aside to avoid a collision.

Although it had sounded like more, there were only six women, one of them Betsy Weston. Some of the others may have been her cabin-mates. I'd had glimpses of two of them before, but these girls were bundled up in mufflers and cardigans against the damp, and in the dimness it was hard to pick out details. It was at that point that I noticed that every light on the ship appeared to be on, but the fog was blotting up the brightness and turning it into a vague glow. I might not have recognized Miss Weston, but she greeted me.

"Mr. Goodale! I'm sorry if my coworkers and I startled you."

Off balance, I blurted out the truth: "Oh, no. I

was just thinking of an idea for my book."

"Great!" she exclaimed. "You must tell me about that, but we do owe you an explanation for charging about the boat deck, laughing like hyenas. We just got messages from both sides of the ocean. The theatre people—the big-shot money men—they've made a deal! We are not going home to unemployment. We're going back to London and the high life. How's that?"

"Wonderful news!" I told her, without reflection on the feelings of my boss.

"Isn't it? Well, take me out for a coffee and tell me about this book. I am interested."

At this point her companions went on their way without her. They were laughing harder than ever.

"See you later!" one of them called.

"Right!" she called back and then switched her attention to me: "And I shall pay for my own coffee. I don't need hand-outs from men, however well-meaning they are."

Oh, dear. I couldn't help feeling that this was a shot against the Honourable Frederick, but, really, she'd doubtless met lots of wealthy chaps, so why should she mean anyone in particular?

She led me to the café in the second class. It wasn't showy, but it was quite nice and homey.

We both got coffees and paid for them separately before we carried them to a table and sat down.

With the rather early hour and the fog, the place wasn't crowded. Betsy opened the conversation.

"Now, then, I have never met an author before, and I don't know anything about it. Where do you get your ideas from?"

I was thoroughly embarrassed. Letting her pay her own way seemed discourteous, but she'd made it clear she wanted it like that. Now she was asking awkward questions and staring at me with her china blue eyes. She hadn't bothered to get dolled up to let off steam with some other girls. Even with her muffler pushed back, her yellow hair was damp and rather straggly. Her cardigan was wet, as well as worn and too faded a blue to set off her eyes. Her skirt was a darker blue and blotched with fog. She looked charmingly real. Well, I couldn't just sit there staring. I had to say something.

"Well, as a matter of fact, in this most recent

effort they seem to arrive one at a time as needed rather than my earlier method of thinking things out properly and taking them down in an orderly fashion."

I wouldn't have thought her eyes could get wider, but they did.

"But is it based on your experiences in real life?" she asked.

"That's difficult to say. Sometimes definitely yes. Then again, not always."

"Give me an example," she urged.

Her rapt attention was certainly flattering.

"Right. Well, I have a villain who needs to hide a body on an ocean liner, and I thought of under the canvas cover of a life boat."

"That could work."

She glanced sideways at a man in a dripping black hat who'd just walked into the café. Then she leaned toward me, as if we were conspiring.

"So I thought at first, but then I discovered that the boats are uncovered for inspection. I'd have to find out if there's a regular schedule for that and, if so, what it is. Oh, good heavens!" I cried. "I've got to get back to my boss. There's something he has to do before we can sail home."

I scrambled to my feet.

"He's not staying in New York?" Betsy frowned.

"No, he's being returned to store, and I go with him. Maybe we could meet later. I could take you dancing," I suggested.

What a dumb thing to say, I reflected at once. I'd just got the bird from someone who didn't dance all that well because my dancing was even worse. Betsy frowned again. I reached out a hand to help her to her feet, not that she needed it; it was just a reflex.

"Please," she replied, "I dance at endless rehearsals and then in the show until my feet are killing me. Why can't someone design comfortable shoes that look good? Can't we just sit and talk? After all, you have such a lot to say, and I'd love to hear all about it."

"But," I reminded her, "you said you liked to dance."

"Well," she replied with a wave of a small, slim hand, "I couldn't do my job, if I hated it, but I do get tired." She gave me a coy smile. "Besides, I couldn't stay in that cabin all the time, and it was safer to see Freddie in public. He used to bribe the band to play waltzes."

He would, I reflected, wishing I'd thought of it.

"All I can do is waltz," I confessed, "and now everyone seems to foxtrot."

She shrugged.

"Fashion. Not long ago, it was the Charleston."

"I can't do that either."

"I can teach you to foxtrot in ten minutes. It's real easy: one reason it's popular, I guess. As you say, you don't really need to know any other dances. People even foxtrot to swing. Anyone can dance. I'd rather listen to you."

"Fine, fine, wonderful!" I agreed in relief. "I'll check with you as soon as I'm free."

Not offering to escort her to her cabin, I took off at a grateful gallop. It felt impolite, but I did have to get back. Once out into the fog I lost speed. It did seem to be thinning out a trifle, or was it my imagination? I'd almost fallen into the error the Honourable had made of taking a dancer dancing, but why hadn't she been frank with him? There must have been other things they could do in public. We were both lucky she'd been frank with me. I did not want to injure the poor dear girl with my huge feet.

Frederick, I could see, really was not suited to this lady. She wanted to talk. He just didn't talk a lot. In the company of a lovely woman, he wanted to smoke and drink and dance. Conclusion: she is not the partner the Honourable wanted her to be. She seemed to like me a bit and be curious about my art—well, writing, anyway. I'd seen no sign that the Honourable had the slightest interest in creativity, and really, that was basically what she lived for. Hey: I'd figured all that out by myself. I must be smart.

Mind awhirl, I arrived back at GHQ to help the Honourable Frederick to dress. He certainly wasn't a great talker, but he didn't need to be. He got his ideas across with few words and the odd imperious hand gesture. Not the person for a cozy chat. He enjoyed my tying his tie for him but did not want anyone shaving him or combing his hair.

When he was properly resplendent he said, "Thank you for your help. Now I need some time to consider a few details about this meeting. You go off for a while and let me think."

That was convenient for me. I went down to the Grill Room for Rowney's rations, or, rather, his grand brunch. I found my pal, the waiter.

If he thought our arrangement strange, he was happy enough to get rich from it.

I hustled back to the Writing Room. One man was leaving. I noted it was not Mirabow but an older man, short, jovial, and rather pudgy. I set to work at the typewriter, which must have been Rowney's dinner bell. I hadn't got down more than a couple of sentences before he strolled in, looking about for the eats. I put down his food— some chicken this time—and the cream and sat back to admire this splendid creature.

After he had cleaned his dishes, he came over to me wanting attention. Then when he'd been satisfactorily petted, he drew off and set about carefully washing his hands and face. Isn't it remarkable how cats do everything in such an orderly manner?

"Oh! That animal is here!" announced a female voice from the doorway.

"Yes, and I love him," I retorted.

Tactfully, Rowney withdrew before this became a vulgar brawl.

"Anyway," Molly said, "I just came to say that I did not mean to be hurtful. I just wanted to make my position clear."

"Oh, quite," I assured her. "I do understand. You were perfectly right, and I respect your honest heart. I truly mean that."

She smiled in her lovely way and moved toward me. Her navy blue, straight-lined dress made her eyes look even more like the sea.

"Who's this?" asked an aristocratic voice behind her. I stood up as he entered the room. "Oh, I think I have seen you before, haven't I?"

"Molly," I said, "this is the Honourable Frederick Oglethorpe, the man I work for. Sir, please let me present Miss Molly Perkins. She's the sister of the elevator operator at your hotel in London."

He bowed.

"Oh, yes, I do remember that chap. Nice boy. So you're part of the ship's company?"

"That's right," she replied, "and must return to my duties before I'm missed."

"Can't you stay and chat, just for a while?"

Said the spider to the fly, I thought to myself. Perfectly turned out and oozing charm: that was the Honourable Frederick. No wonder the lovely labourite wanted to flee.

"No, no, certainly not," she was replying,

edging out the door. "I have things to get done right away."

"Perhaps on another occasion," he suggested. "I'm not going into New York, so we have all the time it takes to get home."

"How nice," she said with a big smile as she hastily disappeared.

CHAPTER
—14—

THE HONOURABLE TURNED TO ME.

"That's the girl who gave you the bird?"

He sounded surprised, I couldn't tell whether at her turning me down or at my ever even making her acquaintance. I suspected the latter.

"Yes, sir. We weren't suited to each other, and she saw it before I did. At any rate, yes, she chucked me."

"Oh, well, if I can get chucked, so can you."

I had to smile a bit. He made it sound as if our drawing the same luck was fair.

"Too true, sir."

"Is there anything I should avoid when talking to her?"

"Well, sir, she doesn't like cats."

"The animal kind?" He raised an eyebrow.

"Yes, sir." I was tempted to let him find out her political views for himself, but that would be petty and spiteful. Besides, she wouldn't keep them a secret long. "She's a great supporter of the labour cause. You know: workers and unions and all that."

"I see." He looked thoughtfully in the direction she'd disappeared. "Possibly I could broaden her views in time. At any rate, why I came to find you was that I've learned we have four hours to wait before the ship docks. When she does, you and I will proceed to the Purser's office and collect our papers. Then we meet the person or persons we hand them over to. Got that?"

I hadn't expected to accompany him on the concluding phase of his mission, but I replied,

"Yes, sir. Quite clear."

"All right. Be back in our stateroom within three hours. There we wait until the actual docking. These men will have boarding passes."

He gave a little salute with his hand and left, probably to return to his pipe but possibly to pursue Molly. I sat down and looked at my typing. What a damned fool I'd been, I realized. Here I was writing a contrived murder mystery with foreign ladies and sinister villains, while all around me was some sort of international big-time stuff, complete with intrigue and genuinely sinister people like Mirabow and even a small-timer like me getting in on the act with my pepper gun. And who was Oglethorpe really? Well, he was a chap the government must trust with a secret document! Wow! What the hell had I been doing? Daydreaming a silly little murder story, and here I was standing on a real story. Not one for the newspapers, of course—no facts or substance—but I could certainly turn the thing I was in the middle of into a first-class, big-time, international sort of story, with a bit added on to include some interesting people I wouldn't even have to make up.

I removed the page I'd been typing and rolled in a clean sheet of paper. No title yet: that would have to come, but I could start off with Rodney being asked by Scotland Yard if he would under-take a certain delicate and, yes, possibly danger-ous mission for them. They regretted that the remuneration would be slender, but he would be helping England. No, by George, he would be helping the British Empire!

As I typed, I forgot to worry about where the keys were. They were just where I needed them to be. If there were a few typographical errors, I could sort them out later. I got seven pages typed and stopped. It was getting close to zero hour. I packed up my stuff, including the priceless manuscript, and returned to our HQ.

In the stateroom the Honourable Frederick hadn't done much to disarrange his sartorial perfection. I brushed off some pipe ash and saw to a few creases and a bit of lint. I was silently amused to find a couple of black cat hairs on his trouser cuffs. Good old Rowney. I noticed that the Honourable had his pocket watch on a gold chain in his vest pocket, and I realized for the first time in my life that I wanted one of those watches, so much more resplendent than an ordinary wrist watch. It makes you look like a somebody.

I did what I could to render the best clothes I had presentable, and I made sure my hair was parted neatly on the left side. I couldn't begin to rival my boss, and it wouldn't be proper to do so, but I didn't want to disgrace him either. He combed his hair one last time. I straightened his tie. We didn't say much. We just walked out into the fog. I'd worried a little about the effect of the damp on our clothes, but the fog had thinned somewhat. From the dock we could see the lights outlining what looked like a large liner passing us on the port side and heading out to sea. I assumed this was the vessel we'd been waiting for to vacate the dock so that we could go in.

We could hear more than see the arrival of tug boats, their small horns beeping about us like boys on bikes moving around a huge lorry. Without hurry we made our way along to the purser's office, where we sat down on some uncomfortable wooden chairs.

We weren't the only ones waiting to retrieve possessions. I was surprised to see nearly sixty men and women queued up, seeking to collect their jewellery or whatever other items they'd considered valuable enough to tempt evil people to purloin them. One of the lady's maids at the table in the dining room had mentioned that some people put things in the purser's safe just to appear important. It seemed like a lot of trouble.

After a long straight run, the ship seemed to sort of stop. No doubt the tugs had kept her in exactly the correct alignment to be docked. There was a hesitation, and then we could hear the ramps thudding down. Those still waiting stirred and muttered impatiently, but not the Honourable Frederick. Even I could see that we were not being rudely neglected. The purser was clearing all the small fry out of the way of the big production.

Nevertheless, I was reminded of a bit of verse I'd run across in school: "And, as the cock crew, those who stood before the tavern shouted, 'Open then the door! You know how little time we have to stay, and once departed, may return no more.'" Something like that, anyway. Of course, the two of us were going to be returning, and Omar Khayyam, so the teacher assured us, was describing souls waiting to be born, but he'd captured perfectly the feeling of queues, I always thought. Rummy licensing laws they must have had in Persia.

Meanwhile, we just sat and waited. I didn't mind. I was avidly collecting really useful material for what I could see was going to be my true international thriller, which no doubt after a brief interval would prove a bestseller. Maybe I could make a pot of money and impress Betsy. No, that was too fanciful. She hadn't been impressed with Oglethorpe's money. I'd guess her dad had plenty, so gold and silver wouldn't win her. On the other hand, the idea of going about with a writer who had made a name for himself might impress her. Slowly, the queue wound to an end.

The phone on the purser's desk made an odd beep. He picked it up.

"Right," he told it. "We are waiting for them. Please send them along."

He stood up and walked over to a small separate safe that I hadn't noticed behind a cupboard in a corner. He entered the combination but remained standing in front of it with the door closed. The Honourable rose. I followed his lead. He drew from his coat pocket a paper that he handed to the purser, who looked it over and then pulled open the safe door. He took out a brown envelope, and I could see on it one of those wax seals like they show you in the movies: The papers! The purser handed the envelope to the Honourable. He took it and nodded.

Right on cue, the expected officials opened the door and walked into the office. Actually, they sort of crowded in. There seemed to be more than the four there really were. The leading man was a smartly dressed chap with a high-class turn-out nearly as good as my boss. A step behind him came another not quite so elegant and behind them two New York police-men, the first I'd ever seen in the flesh. They wore uniforms like postmen but carried guns at their sides: real American coppers.

"I'm Arthur Jollet," the leading man announced, "assistant to our ambassador in Washington."

He was a largish chap with a bit of grey hair left on an otherwise bald head, gold-rimmed spectacles, a reddish face, and a very good black cane with ivory at the ends. He held up toward us a leather wallet open to some sort of identifi-cation thing.

The next chap in civilian rig was younger and less well dressed, quite ordinary looking. He also held up a leather case with a photo of himself, etc.

He said, "I'm Walter Painter. I'm just along to help, if needed."

He didn't have to explain. It didn't take a second glance to see the toughness under the bland façade. He was no doubt armed.

Mr. Jollet continued: "The mayor of New York insisted on sending along two of his policemen to help us, if needed, and we certainly appreciate such kindness on his part."

Intimidated—even, I admit, a little scared—I tried to melt into the background, but Mr. Oglethorpe smiled, introduced himself and me without other explanation, and shook hands with Mr. Jollet and Mr. Painter. Although I shrank back, they insisted on shaking hands with me as well. The Honourable did not tell them that I was just a valet and that they'd soiled themselves shaking mitts with the help. The obvious assumption was that I was his bodyguard, a tough, like Painter. I found my feelings about that rather mixed.

With an apologetic air, the Honourable Frederick took from his inside coat pocket a photo of Mr. Jollet and a photo of his signature. He had Mr. Jollet sign for the documents, and before he handed them over, he compared the signature and the photo he'd been given. He nodded his satisfaction and placed the documents into the hands of Mr. Jollet, who nodded back. With smiles all around, the official party and armed guards withdrew from our presence. For a few moments we both stood there like runners at the end of one of those marathon things, thoroughly tired. An old campaigner, the Honourable recovered first. He squared his shoulders, gave me a reassuring smile, and thanked the purser. Then we drifted back to the stateroom.

My employer resumed his chair and picked up his pipe. I remained standing, awaiting further orders. After he'd blown into his pipe a few times, he looked up at me with a frown.

"Oh, do sit down, Goodale!" he bade me.

"Very good, sir," I replied, obeying.

"Look," he said, "I've been meaning to ask you: do you mind if I take this former girlfriend of yours out? If you do, say so."

I blinked at him.

"No, sir," I could reply honestly. "We were never all that close. I definitely have no claim on that lady. She is a nice, good-hearted young woman with more intelligence than many would think, but she is not for me. I am not distressed— far from it, I assure you. I wish you well."

"Scout's honour?" he pressed, holding up a hand with three fingers extended.

I returned the salute and assured him, "Scout's honour. Now," I ventured hesitantly, "I return the question, and I feel silly and rather forward as a valet asking this, but I've discovered that I like Miss Weston. Do you have a problem with that? You seemed quite attached to her for a while."

"Oh, I was, but she kicked the props out from under my affection. I am out of that, and after seeing Handsome Molly, I'm happy to be free to go after her.'"

"Well, the best of luck, sir."

"And you." We exchanged a rather rueful smile. "Who'd believe the things that happen aboard ship, eh? Changing partners like in an old country dance." He shook his head. "What care I for gold and silver? All I want is a handsome man."

"Sir? Is that Shakespeare?"

"No. My old nurse."

They seemed to have odd servants on the Oglethorpe estate.

"Oh. May I get you anything?"

"Not at the moment. Go have a bit of a lie down."

Accordingly, I retired to my room. Left alone, my brain started to digest my recent experiences, and it hit me: Jollet was perfect for my real villain. Magellan would do for an ordinary cut-throat or a hired gunman, but I needed a master criminal behind the scenes, working the big game. Jollet would become Doktor Blasfeemer, the spider at the centre of the complex web of International Intrigue and all that sort of stuff.

I thought about that for a while and then decided to go do some typing, but the boss needed me again.

"Look," he said, "I want to send Miss Perkins a note. Would you find out if Winterhaiter is available, and, if so, send him to me. When does she get off duty?"

"Well, sir, I have no positive knowledge of her job as such, but with passengers disembarking and a bunch of new ones coming aboard, she may have to work longer than usual."

I met Winterhaiter coming along to our state-room, carrying the box I had had Joe the carpenter make for me.

"Ah, just the chap!" I greeted him. "My thanks to you, and I have another job. Please see the Honourable Frederick and collect a note from him to take to Miss Molly Perkins, wherever she may be."

I took the box. He nodded and went off to collect the note and no doubt a refresher, as the men of law call it. I stuck my head into the Writing Room. To my surprise, two women had chosen this time to write postcards. Perhaps they'd promised to send them from the Princess Alexandra, and this was their last chance. I didn't see Rowney anywhere.

I returned to the centre of the vortex to put the box into my room and see what I was to do next.

The Honourable didn't seem to notice my strange box.

He sort of wandered about for a bit and then said, "Oh, I won't be needing you anymore. Why don't you go off and learn to play quoits or something? And please remember to call first."

"Very good, sir."

Presumably he didn't need me to straighten his tie. I took off on winged feet for the boat deck. I liked it there, and I still needed a good place on a liner to hide a corpse. I mean, if you have a perfectly good ocean liner under your feet, why wouldn't you use it in your story? Right?

I was strolling about, looking at the still-swirling fog and what were probably new passengers, when a woman's voice said, "Well, Rodney, are you going to pass me by without a word?"

I was rather surprised—no, shocked—that I was so far gone in my story that I had missed this girl in the fog. The visibility had improved a lot in the course of the day.

"Oh, I am sorry, truly I am! To tell you the truth, I'm on to a great bunch of characters, and the plot is beginning to form. Straight goods! I've got a terrific master criminal who almost writes the story for me."

"Is that possible?" Miss Weston exclaimed. "I mean, I have no idea about this sort of thing, but it sounds so strange."

"Not at all strange, really. Lots of writers have

their stories dictated by their characters. They sort of make it happen. Because of the way they are, they go in a set direction. You can start with a plot, but then you need to come up with characters who will do what you need done."

I must have sounded like a writer with decades of experience. Well, I was a writer, and the experience was real; it just came from Ann Merrit's book and the people I'd listened to at the Frozen Inkpot. I was discovering that they'd all been right.

"It sounds like living in your head," she declared, wide-eyed.

"Well, I never thought about it that way, but it does sort of work out as you say."

"Let's get a coffee at that same café place we went to before," she urged.

"Right ho" I agreed. "This time I pay."

"No," the fair lady decreed, "we each pay for our own."

"Oh, really now, here I am with more of my own money than I have ever had at one time, and I can't spend it on the lady of my dreams."

She coloured slightly, making her look even prettier.

"I hope they are nice dreams," she murmured.

"I like them."

"That's not quite the same thing," she objected, "but we shall let that pass for the present."

As we talked, she'd been moving toward the café, towing me along with her by an apparently effortless magic. Inside, we got a table easily. The new passengers would be sorting their stuff out in their cabins, so they would not be needing coffees yet.

We got ours and sat looking at each other. With a flowered dress, she was wearing a small sort of pinned-on hat with a fan of light blue feathers on one side. A few drops of moisture from the fog outside glistened on it like diamonds. It really set off her eyes beautifully. I suppose she knew that. I'd never given too much thought to my appearance myself, but she being a woman, and moreover a woman in show business, her care for how she looked would be doubled in spades. Still, when I was a valet delivering another man's message, I'd seen her before she'd got ready to go out. She hadn't had the magic of perfection but an even more appealing softness.

I could not believe what had happened, and

all without my even worrying or being confused or afraid of saying the wrong thing. It was just unfolding, as if it were a play. We made up the lines, and it was just right.

"Here's the thing I wanted to talk about," she told me.

"Yes, go on," I prompted, eager to learn what would come next.

"I thought you English people always drank tea."

Taken by surprise, I couldn't help laughing. This puzzled her, but she smiled back.

"I do sometimes, but I do like coffee, when it's properly made. American coffee is good. The stuff I had in Paris was awful. Was that what you wanted to talk about?"

"No, not really. It just crossed my mind." She hesitated, then continued: "When we reach London—how do we get in touch with each other?"

That had taken her some effort. She was accustomed to men asking her questions like that. I gave her my most reassuring smile.

"Good point. A—yes, we are both going to London. B—I assume I will be at the same hotel as my boss. He has rooms rented there, sort of all the time, what they call a permanent guest."

"OK," she nodded. "Now, being a writer, I assume you have a pen and paper."

I drew them out with the flourish of a magician doing a trick.

"Very adroit," she commended. "Now please write the name of the hotel and the street it's on. I don't know where I'll be staying, but I can phone you there. I will phone first, not just turn up. Then we can get together, and you can show me around London."

"I would love to, but I don't actually come from there, so we can discover its marvels together."

"Even more fun. Do you have to get back to work soon?"

"No, the boss kicked me out. He's going to take Molly Perkins dancing, etc. Funny, isn't it? She was the girl I was going after, but it didn't pan out. She said I lacked pizzazz."

"Freddie will give her plenty of that." She dropped her gaze. "You were waiting for me to show up, and I did."

"Yes, indeed," I nodded.

"It's funny we should meet at all. I should be

back in East Islip."

"What an odd name! Where is it?"

"Not all that far from here. On Long Island. It is a silly name. It sounds like it should be an Indian word. It could mean something like 'big houses near water.' They told us in school, though, that one of the early settlers named it after where he'd come from in England, so it's really all your fault." She smiled reminiscently. "When we were kids, we used to say it was where a monkey had stepped on a banana peel and said, 'Ooh, I slip!' I bet you haven't even seen the show, have you?"

"Well—no," I confessed. "I was in Paris for six months, and I came back broke. I heard it was great, though, and I saw the interview in the paper with your picture. It didn't do you justice."

That was always safe to tell girls.

"When we get back to London, I'll slip you into one of the press seats. You are a writer. I'm the star's friend—one of them, anyway. I have eight lines and one good speech, and I sing the title song. That's pretty good, don't you think?"

"It's terrific, especially for someone so young. You must have a lot of talent."

How could the Honourable dismiss her as

a mere show girl? Macbeth might have to wait awhile, but she was on her way.

She told me a little about her dad's boat business and how upset her mother was about her theatrical ambitions. She was her dad's second wife and so always came in for criticism from the family of the first. I talked about the farm my father had bought up north after he decided he'd never become admiral in peacetime. He didn't need to make money at it, so he could just enjoy playing farmer.

"That sounds nice," she remarked. "I like animals."

"Cats?"

"Oh, yes."

"But not dogs?"

"Well, not as much. Big dogs scare me. Do you like them?"

"Some of them. You have to get to know them."

"Like people."

We had a few coffees, and suddenly it was rather late.

"Please, just let me call in to see if I'm wanted," I requested.

"You go ahead, but to tell the truth, I'm sleepy, despite the coffee. Things have really turned around for me, and I haven't caught up to myself yet," she stated apologetically.

I called the head office and got the coded reply, "Please come home, Aunt Zelda."

I returned to Betsy and said, "I have to clock in, anyway. You know, from now on I'm going to call you Liz."

She smiled a huge smile. It made her look very young.

"Well, good for you. My coworkers call me Betsy, and so did my school friends. Maybe a slight change of the old handle is exactly what is needed to help things along in the right direction."

"Good. Well, I shall return you to your cabin and then go to mine."

"Right-ho, as you limeys say."

Outside her cabin we kissed good night without saying anything.

She slipped in. I could hear some giggles from the other girls, but I couldn't care less, and she could put it down to envy.

CHAPTER
—16—

Back in first class the Honourable Frederick met me at the door and said, "Come in, and sit down. Things are going to be altered, and it all starts here and now."

Oh, dear, I thought. I might have known everything was going too well. What now?

I suppose my apprehension showed , because he went on: "No, nothing to worry about. We just need to adjust matters so we shall both be more comfortable and better off." He sat down, and I rather warily followed his example. "From now on you are my secretary, and you get two pounds per week—but I'll still need you to tie my ties for a while. Understood?"

"Yes, sir," I replied, stunned. "Thank you."

"Well, then, let us both have a double brandy and soda and then hit the hay. The ship leaves for home early tomorrow morning, rain or shine, and I don't want to be awake for it."

He carried out his threat of the brandy and soda doubles, and after a sketchy bit of getting ready, we did hit the so-called hay. I'd never got around to eating dinner, and I'm not used to doubles. I went out like a light.

When I woke up next morning, it took a few minutes to recall the momentous happenings of the previous day. The Honourable wasn't up yet. Since he'd said he wanted to sleep in, I just went down to get a piece of beef and some cream for Rowney. I met up with the cat hanging about the empty Writing Room, clearly annoyed at having to wait for me, but after he'd eaten, he condescended to sit on me for a while. Then he ran off to attend to important cat business that no doubt required his urgent attention.

Out on deck it was raining very heavily. I decided not to go for a walk. When I returned to the stateroom, I found the boss just barely awake. I slipped him a cup of tea and ordered us a larger breakfast than usual. He came to and got sorted out with no assistance from me this time. I stayed handy but out of his way. No ties yet.

When breakfast arrived, I helped the man in with the food, set it down on the table, and passed the chap tuppence as a mark of my new status. I was a bit concerned that the Honourable would consider such a lot of food first thing in the morning uneconomical, but he ate nearly as much as I did, so I was glad I had ordered it. Soon it was all gone with barely a word said except, "Thanks," when I passed the marmalade.

"Right-ho," he said, as he sat back, replete, and picked up his pipe. "Now we come to the actual substance of your new job."

"Yes, sir," I said quietly.

"Yes." He reached into a drawer. "I have here some pages of mine that should be typed out. I have been told that they like things in writing, but what they really mean is typed and signed," he grumbled, then went on: "So go to it, and let's see how you do. I did observe you typing, so you can, correct?"

"Yes, sir. I see no reason why this should be a

problem," said the big-mouthed, over-confident clown. "I'll get to it at once."

"Sorry about using your paper. I didn't bring any myself."

"Oh, there's lots, and I'm sure I can get more on the ship. Winterhaiter can help me."

I went to the Writing Room. Ignoring the small fry with their silly cards and letters, I sat down at my accustomed typewriter. This was big stuff, I thought, as I rolled in my first piece of paper.

Then I actually looked at the first page of the document. Oh, my God, the writing was awful! That is, it looked very nice, almost like drawing, in fact, but I couldn't read a word of it. I could only assume that it must be in English. Between his eccentric handwriting and the broad-nibbed pen he'd used, well, this was going to be like code-breaking. I squared my shoulders and got down to it. I was not going to fail at my first job for him, and that was that.

Then I got an idea: code-breaking. I would treat this like code-breaking. I sat there and looked down the page until I found a word I thought I could read. I could crack it! This gave me clues as to what vague mark meant which letter of the alphabet. Slowly, I worked my way through, copying it out. When I finished a page, I typed it up. The task got easier as I went along.

I got an idea for my arch-villain, Blasfeemer. What if he could break the government's coded messages and use them to his own evil ends, such as being able to take out an official courier? Hmm.

I pushed on with the job until I had finished the last page and left a place for him to sign and date it. When I read it over, it did make sense— disappointingly boring sense, but sense. A little voice in my head said, "I always win." I wondered what it was on about this time.

Carefully, I picked up all the papers before I left the room, sorting out the copies from the pages. When I got back to him, he was still messing about with his pipe.

"This isn't drawing right!" he complained. "Damn it! This is a DeGingham pipe, the best in London! Hell—in the world!"

I waited for him to subside and then handed him the good copy of his documents. He read the papers through and signed them. Then he looked up the date on his pocket calendar thing and added it. I decided I should buy one of those, along with the pocket watch.

"What took you so long?"

"I had to wait for a machine," I adroitly lied.

"Oh, right. I forgot that anyone can use them. When we get back, I'll have to get you one of your own. You didn't have any trouble with my writing, did you? Of course not! What a fuss about nothing! Those machines make people lazy. Before you know it, everyone will have forgotten how to write. Bloody pipe!" he muttered. "Do me a favour and find the steward—Winterhaiter? Really. What a name! I want him to take a note to Molly."

"She'd be at work, sir," I pointed out.

"But I want to see her when she gets off work. Sort it out for me. There's a good chap."

I went out. Of course, so early in the voyage everyone was busy. After some effort I found the culprit and passed him the note for the pretty Molly. Then I went back and sat down, feeling I wasn't doing enough.

At least the Honourable Frederick had stopped cursing his pipe. It looked to me as if he were smoking a different one, but I was hardly an expert. He gazed at me for a minute with a sort of concerned expression and then said, "That strange box thing is for the cat Molly takes exception to."

This was a statement, not a question.

"Yes, sir," I replied a bit sheepishly.

"Fine. You want to take the cat ashore with you. Where to?"

"Well, sir, I was thinking I could take him up to my folks' farm. It is a long way, but –"

"Right. Well, I have a solution—a better idea. Now, listen. I have a three-storey building I own on Eustace Street, not too far from the hotel. Now the downstairs is empty, vacated by the law office that was there. It will become more offices or a shop of some kind. At present there's a watchman there. I need the upstairs covered, too. When we get to London, I want you and the feline to move in there. I will get keys and all that sorted out before we get to town. The watchman can let you in. I shall ring him up once we are ashore."

It sort of sounded like: now the 3rd Brigade will attack on this line while the divisional artillery lays down a barrage on the enemy gun positions and first line trenches.

"Pardon me, sir," I ventured very politely, "but were you an officer in the war?"

"Well, yes, I was," he granted, "but only for the last year. Why?"

"Oh, it just crossed my mind. An idle question, nothing more," I assured him.

It did fit with the military books.

He nodded with a bit of a frown. I had interrupted his train of thought.

"Well, at any rate, that is covered. Now: the next thing is a few business letters for you to type. We can mail them as soon as we land."

He pulled out five of the things and gave them to me. I thought it would show a lack of confidence if I spared them more than a glance. Thank God, none of them looked very long. I got myself together, put the letters into my pocket, and went off to get Rowney more to eat. Then I sat down at the typewriter. I could have used some lunch myself by then, but I daren't waste the time. Fortunately, I found I could start typing almost at once. I was getting used to my boss's handwriting.

Rowney came in. He said hello and then

started in on his chicken and cream. With one corner of my mind I was formulating a plan to get him into the travelling box.

"It'll be all right, Rowney," I assured him. "It's only for a few hours, not for a day or more after all. We'll be living together in our own London flat. Won't that be nice? Who knows? Maybe there'll be mice."

Fortunately, I had no humans around to consider me crazy. They were probably all at lunch.

I gathered from the letters I was typing that the Honourable Frederick owned a number of properties, mostly in London, which he rented out: not an impecunious younger son, then. It hadn't occurred to me that this would be a logical business—and income—for some of the well-off folk.

A vision of loveliness appeared at the door. She'd done something to her fair hair that made it look like a crown, and she wore a baby blue cardigan over a striped blue-and-white dress that showed off her shapely legs.

"Hard at work?" she smiled.

Taken by surprise, I sort of stammered, "Miss Weston! I mean Betsy! I mean Liz!"

I felt stupid, but she looked pleased, so I guess it was all right.

"Don't let me interrupt you. I only have a minute right now, but I want to have dinner with you at that Grill Room place. Please let me know when you will be available. I'm going to be going over our costumes. We just packed them away anyhow; we didn't think we'd need them again, and now they have to be ready, all pressed and mended and repacked. So I'm off."

And she vanished.

I sat stunned. Rowney emerged from under the desk. I'd forgotten he was still there. After a rub against my leg, off he wandered, and I got back to work. The ship increased her speed. I supposed we must have hit the open water. I realized that I rather liked being on a ship. Yes, I could now understand my dad's feelings about it more easily.

CHAPTER
— 17 —

I took the letters to the Honourable. He read them through and nodded.

"Fine."

"Sir? Do you suppose I could have the evening off?" I ventured.

He chuckled.

"You're taking it off whether you want it or not."

He sent Winterhaiter off with a note for Molly. I gave him one for Liz. From the speed of the replies, the ladies hadn't had to think over their responses.

"Right," the Honourable pronounced. "You get done up yourself and do my tie. Then off you go to your girl and me to mine."

Again, it sounded like a staff conference at the front.

He had no need to hurry me off. I really wanted to see Liz as soon as I could. She'd given me a time to meet her at the Grill Room, and I made sure I was early, even though Molly had always been a trifle late, not much, just five or ten minutes. I'd heard that was considered proper for ladies.

Well, Liz was dead on time. Probably, I thought, it was: A. her naval background, or B. her experience in the theatre, where everything is so carefully timed. One day I might find out more about that. At present I was too inwardly happy to care about a trifle.

"Boy," she greeted me in her filmy red gown, "you are always dead on time, aren't you? I like that in a fella. That was one thing that Freddie had, too."

"Oh, really?"

I felt that she must have been seeing my thoughts.

"Yeah. There's nothing more off-putting, especially at the start of a relationship, than the guy being late. It's hard to believe he cares."

"Well, I was brought up to pay attention to those things, and the Honourable was an army officer, but, really, I was just eager to see you again,"

Liz turned rather pinker than usual and dropped her eyes.

"Shall we go in?" I urged.

Confronted with the menu, I remarked to Liz, "You must have been taken to a lot of fancy places. Do you know what all these French dishes are?"

She laughed.

"No, not all of them. After I found out what a couple really were, I stopped asking. Actually, though, if it says something clear, like beef or chicken, and then something French, it usually means it's in some sort of sauce, and it's often pretty good. I think, though, I'd like the roast turkey."

"Yes," I agreed. "What a good idea. I've heard they have good port. We can have that with the turkey, can't we?"

"I'd like to see anyone try to stop us. Not a whole bottle, though, okay?"

After we'd ordered, there was a lull in the conversation.

"You know," she reflected, "since I've been on board I think I do sort of understand more what my dad felt for the Navy and the sea and all that."

If I'd been eating, I would have choked. This was getting dangerous. Liz was so close to me I could not get away. What was more, I had no desire to. This must be what they meant by "soul-mates." Scary.

"Yes," I told her, "I've found that, too." I rather hurried to change the subject. "Oh, I'm not a valet anymore."

Liz's face fell.

"Freddie didn't fire you, did he?"

"No, he promoted me. I'm now his secre-tary—at two pounds a week, with a London flat of my own."

"Oh, Rodney!" she cried. "That's wonderful! I mean, I know it's your writing that's the impor-tant thing, but it can take so long to get estab-lished in a field, and you don't want to waste your energy worrying about the rent, do you?"

"No, definitely not," I agreed.

"Is he a good boss, really?" she probed.

"Oh, yes," I assured her. Picking my words, I continued, "He's interesting."

She made a face.

"I guess that's one way of putting it. I thought he was a nut, but, then, I don't understand you English. I'm used to rich guys who find chorus girls exciting and make promises they forget about in the morning. You learn pretty quick how to deal with that, let me tell you. Freddie's scary. He really is. Did they make you read *Jane Eyre* in school?"

"No, I don't think so," I confessed.

"Oh, you'd remember, if they had. Mr. Rochester is Freddie to a tee. Domineering. Hypnotic, even." She shook herself. "You say no, just to prove you still can. You don't suppose he's—well, really dangerous?"

I burst out laughing. I couldn't help it.

"I'm serious, Rodney," Liz protested.

I took her hand.

"Yes, I know, and I'm sorry, if my boss frightened you. It's just that he's used to telling people what to do."

"Is he ever! I absolutely could not make him understand that, yes, it's not always easy or pleasant, being a chorus girl, but there are good times, too. Besides, if you want to get into the theatre, you have to start somewhere, don't you?"

"Of course," I agreed, "and you really do want a career in the theatre."

I tried not to make that a question.

"Oh, yes, I do. I don't know if I'll ever get to play Lady Macbeth, but no one will hire you for a good, fat role until you've proven yourself in bit parts, and you don't get even those right away. I have spent a lot of time auditioning."

We ate our meal slowly, drank a little port, and talked. The evening was well advanced when I got around to ringing up our stateroom to ask if I should return. The message was not in code.

He just said, "Sure. Fine."

I knew something was up. Reluctantly, I rather hurried Liz along back to her cabin. We did have a kissing match outside her door. In my haste afterward I only realized as I walked into the stateroom that I must have lip rouge all over my face.

I came to an abrupt halt as I saw that Freddie had the same colour scheme as I had, only rather darker. We both started to laugh. I firmly put the brakes on in my head. I had to myself called him Freddie, and that was a no-no.

"You are going to be the first person I tell," he said.

"Yes, sir?" I replied, waiting.

"Molly and I are going to be married when we get home."

I was rather taken aback, but I said, "Congratulations," and offered my hand. He grabbed it and squeezed it a bit too hard. He was stronger than I'd supposed.

"Yes," he said. "I wanted to have the wedding aboard the ship, but she said no, her folks should be there, and she wanted to impress her girlfriends, so I said fine, we'd do it her way."

A bit sudden, I thought. Then I realized that, if Liz and I had thought of it, we might be doing the same thing. Well, I didn't want to rush her. I might frighten her off, if I tried, and I couldn't risk that.

Having washed the ladies' makeup from our faces and sorted ourselves out, we went to bed. I expected to be too keyed up to sleep, but I was also very tired, and dozed off at once.

At daybreak—well, about eleven in the

morning—I was awakened by a decided knock on the door of the stateroom. Putting on my dressing gown, I went and opened it. There stood a largish chap in a ship's officer's uniform, blue for the Atlantic run. I didn't recognize him.

"Are you the Honourable Frederick Oglethorpe?" he demanded in official tones.

"No, I'm his secretary. As far as I know, he's still asleep. May I help you?" I replied, a bit taken aback by his formal manner.

"Please inform him that the captain wishes to see him in his cabin as soon as possible."

"Very good, sir," I agreed. "I shall so inform him."

He wheeled and marched off. I closed the door behind him and went to see the boss. He was now awake—he could hardly have helped it. Sitting up in bed, he looked inquiringly at me.

"The captain wants to see you, sir, as soon as you can make it."

"Isn't English a wonderful language?" he yawned. "Oh, well, he'll see me at my convenience. Order tea and crumpets for us, and let's get dressed to meet this person."

"You haven't met him at dinner, sir?"

"Not really. I sat at his table a couple of times, but I can't say I know him."

He was fishing for his slippers. I found them for him and then left to order breakfast. He did not hurry dressing, so I kept pace with him easily, while giving him what little assistance he ever required. No one had asked me to go along, but I intended to, unless stopped.

I did select a wide-ish black tie for him and put it on with the right side a shade shorter than the left for that casual effect. We took our time over our tea and left the stateroom together. I told myself that, as his secretary, I should be present at any important meeting. I guess I was right.

At least the boss didn't order me back. A whole new set of duties for me to learn. I hoped I wouldn't muck it up.

Upon our arrival, we were ushered at once into the Big Chief's office. His name was Orbiton; it was in gold letters on the door. He rose from his desk, but he didn't offer to shake hands, nor did the Honourable Frederick. The Captain was slighter in build than I'd expected, sallow of complexion, and unhappy-looking.

"I would have dealt with this sooner," he

began, "but I have had a lot to look after, with the state of the weather and some technical trouble with the ship, nothing to worry about. The point is that there has been a complaint lodged."

"Indeed?" replied the Honourable in a cold, official-sounding voice. "A complaint against whom?"

"A man in your employ, Mr. Rodney Goodale. Is this the one?"

I nodded.

"What is the complaint," my boss demanded, "and who made it?"

The temperature in the room had dropped perceptibly. Most sailors have reddish faces from the weather. Captain Orbiton's turned an interesting shade of maroon.

"Mr. Jon Mirabow claims that this man Goodale blew pepper into his face in order to force his way into his cabin." He eased back his formal manner a trifle. "He says he doesn't know why, but he was very upset when he left the ship at New York. Additional inquiries I made lead me to believe that Goodale had used one of my crew to help him in this business, a steward named Winterhaiter."

At this cue, probably because Orbiton had pressed a signal button, the man Winterhaiter was escorted into the room by a ship's officer, who then left. I expected the steward to be wearing handcuffs, in addition to an understandably dismayed expression. The Honourable did not even glance at him. He concentrated his frozen glare on the captain, who seemed almost as unhappy.

"Now I know you had some kind of official business here," he conceded, "but your man has to be held answerable for assault, forcible entry, and I don't know what else. I'll have to ask the purser."

"That's enough of this," snapped the Honourable Frederick. "I ordered the so-called assault on Mr. Barberpole, or whatever his name was."

"You did?" Orbiton exclaimed. "Then you are responsible!"

"Of course I am." *You fool* was loudly unspoken.

"Then I should have you arrested and confined to your stateroom until we dock and I can turn you over to the police in Southampton."

"You take any action against any of us, and I

shall see to it that His Majesty's government does not loan the D&W Shipping Line a shilling of what they asked for, and I shall inform them that you are the cause of the end of D&W," the Honourable Frederick told him coldly and quietly.

Blimey! The financial trouble of the big shipping lines in the Depression had been front-page news.

"Now see here!"

The captain tried to regain control of the situation, but he'd lost the reins on the far turn.

"No. You see here. These men acted out of patriotic motives. They did what they did for England—no, damn it, for the Empire! And you get in the way. You should be ashamed of your conduct."

The captain was by now a deep purple. You really had to feel sorry for the man.

He said, "Now that I am acquainted with the true facts, of course I withdraw the complaint. It did seem strange—With no apparent motive—perhaps a joke—I had no way of knowing this was so important. I do hope that a private apology from me will do. Such a sensitive matter."

The Honourable Frederick glared as if he

intended to prosecute the war, but then he relented and said: "A natural misunderstanding. Let us put it behind us. I assure you that Mr. Winterhaiter has had no concern either with any wrong-doing. He acted merely for his king and country."

In fact, he'd done nothing whatever except his job, but this sounded a lot better.

"Of course, of course," Captain Orbiton agreed. "Please just forget the entire thing."

The Honourable Frederick nodded, and we three conspirators all filed out of the office. Winterhaiter disappeared with amazing speed, compounded no doubt of a desire to be out of the way of any official changes of mind and an eagerness to tell his mates the story. They'd listen, but they wouldn't believe a word. Plump little Winterhaiter involved in high government intrigue? No, nobody would fall for that story.

When we'd arrived back in the stateroom, I couldn't contain my surprise and admiration:

"I didn't realize you had so much pull, sir!"

"Listen, Goodale: you have as much pull as you can convince the other chap you have."

CHAPTER
—18—

As the RMS Princess Alexandra docked at Southampton, the Royal Air Force Band began to play a welcome for some bigwig I hadn't even known was on board. Two big, black, official-looking limousines met us as we disembarked. The new couple went off in the first, Molly smiling up at the Honourable Frederick. Drivers were supplied by the company; Molly wouldn't be disturbed, at least by her fiancé's driving. Rowney and I went in the second. We were heading for London. For the time being he was furious with me, but he'd get over it. Cats are opportunists.

I'd given my new address to Liz so she could find me. She'd be pretty busy at first, what with having to come up with new lodgings and the show reopening. She seemed to be an unofficial petty officer with the troop. She was very good at telling people what to do.

One of my first tasks in London as the Honourable Frederick's secretary would be to teach his brother-in-law, Bill Perkins, how to tie his ties properly. The Honourable was passing my valet job on to the elevator boy. I supposed valet was a step up, but I thought I'd figured out why he went through so many valets: it was how he got to know men. If he could use them somewhere in his little financial empire, he promoted them. If he couldn't, he went on to the next one.

The watchman let me into my new home. It was quite big and rather empty. I'd have to write to my folks. I wasn't in the Navy, true, but I did have a proper job. I closed the door and opened the box. Rowney leapt out before I could change my mind , and he began to inspect the place.

"Rowney," I told him, "you are now king of all you survey."

He flicked his ears in acceptance.

The wedding date was set. The ceremony took place at St. George's, Hanover Square, on the

31ˢᵗ of the month. Although all brides are pretty, Molly glowed in yards and yards of ivory-coloured lace that must have taken awhile to make. I was best man.

Waiting for the photographer to set his camera up, the boss and I were standing together off to one side on the steps outside the church.

On impulse, I asked him straight out: "What were the documents we took across to the States?"

"How the hell should I know? I'm just the paperboy."

EPILOGUE

I'VE FINALLY GOT NEW SHOES AND A GOOD SUIT—
and a gold pocket watch and a pocket calendar,
but the main thing everyone will want to know
about is the novel. Well, in *The Atlantic Liner
Mystery,* Inspector Rodney not only solves the
crime but then is appointed head of a new
Scotland Yard department in charge of crimes
on board passenger liners. It sold 100,000
copies, some of which I signed. I haven't bought
my ivory-tipped cane yet.